"Tonig... a last fling."

Carly made a hopeless gesture. "But it's over, and I'm going to forget it."

She moved to hurry away, but Kyle caught her wrist. "You can't just walk away. Your whole future could depend on what you decide now."

"I've already decided." Carly glared at him angrily. "I don't want to get involved."

"Will you kiss me goodbye?"

The color fled from her face, and she stared at him, unable to speak.

"You see? You're already involved." He suddenly let go of her wrist. "Run away if you must. But you'll be back."

Carly tried to deny it, but no words came out. Turning on her heel, she ran for the safety of her flat as if all the Viking hordes were after her.

Books by Sally Wentworth

HARLEQUIN PRESENTS

HARLEQUIN ROMANCES

These books may be available at your local bookseller.

For a list of all titles currently available,
send your name and address to:

Harlequin Reader Service
P.O. Box 52040, Phoenix, AZ 85072-2040
Canadian address: P.O. Box 2800, Postal Station A,
5170 Yonge St., Willowdale, Ont. M2N 5T5

SALLY
WENTWORTH

viking invader

Harlequin Books

TORONTO • NEW YORK • LONDON
AMSTERDAM • PARIS • SYDNEY • HAMBURG
STOCKHOLM • ATHENS • TOKYO • MILAN

Harlequin Presents first edition December 1984
ISBN 0-373-10750-1

Original hardcover edition published in 1984
by Mills & Boon Limited

CHAPTER ONE

'HEY! Hey, you!'

Carly Morgan looked up from her sketch pad and saw that a man was shouting in her direction from a boat on the river. She glanced behind her, but there was no one else near by. Getting to her feet, she put her pad and pencil down on the bench and walked the few yards to the river's edge. 'Do you mean me?' she called back.

'Yes, of course I mean you. Who else is there? Here, catch this rope!'

Without giving her any time to prepare herself, the man threw the rope coiled in his hands and it snaked across the river towards her. The only way Carly caught it was because it more or less fell into her hands and she automatically grabbed it. And it was wet, she noticed with distaste; drips flew off it on to her face and clothes.

'Okay, I've got it.' She looked round, wishing that there were some of the schoolboys who always fished along the bank who could take the rope from her, but they all seemed to have disappeared this evening.

'Well, don't just stand there, woman!' the boatman shouted at her exasperatedly. 'Haul me in!'

Carly's mouth tightened grimly; she wasn't used to being spoken to in that tone, but she obediently pulled on the horrible rope, shaking considerably more water on herself in the process. The boat was one of those old-fashioned long, narrow barges that used to be used as working boats along the canals of England in the nineteenth and early twentieth centuries but are now mostly used as pleasure craft. It was brightly painted in

5

black and red with the name *Lydia* on the side surrounded by the traditional painted swags of flowers. It also looked very heavy. Carly tugged on the rope and felt considerable surprise when the boat started to come in to the bank.

'Don't walk backwards with it!' the man shouted. 'Pull it in hand over hand.' And then, as she obeyed, 'Good girl. Keep going!'

When the back end of the boat was about a yard from the bank, he jumped easily ashore, another rope in his hands. 'Hang on to your rope,' he instructed her in passing, 'while I make the bow fast.'

Rather indignantly, Carly stayed where she was, watching while he ran along the bank to opposite the front of the boat, hauled it in by his rope, then took a metal stake and a hammer from his belt, and made the rope fast to the stake when he'd hammered it into the ground. Then he ran back to Carly, hammered in another stake almost at her feet and, taking the rope from her, tied that one up as well. Then he straightened up. 'Good,' he grunted. 'I was beginning to think I'd drift down the river for miles before I found anyone.'

Carly found herself looking up at a veritable giant of a man in his late twenties or early thirties, face tanned and with eyes of an incredibly clear blue, bluer than the summer sky. He was wearing only sandals and a pair of ragged denim shorts, leaving bare his broad chest, covered by a mat of hairs that gleamed gold in the evening sun. There was a sweat band round his head and he was either trying to grow a beard or hadn't bothered to shave for a couple of weeks.

He grinned at her, looking her over in frank appreciation, his blue eyes travelling the length of her tall, slender figure in a fashionable layered skirt in shades of green with a top that came up high in the front but was cut low at the back. 'Thanks for catching the rope. Something got caught round the prop and the engine stalled.'

Deciding that in the circumstances she'd forgive him his high-handedness, Carly nodded, 'That's okay,' and began to walk back to the bench.

'Hey, don't run away. I still need help to free my prop.'

'But surely you can do that by yourself?' Carly protested.

The blond giant shook his head. 'It's a two-man job.'

'Then I suggest you find a man to help you,' she retorted tartly.

'But there isn't anyone else around,' he pointed out with an expressive wave of his hand. Then, persuasively, 'All I want you to do is to pass me a few tools. You're not going to leave me stranded, are you?' he added with a smile.

It was rather a nice smile, despite the unshaven chin, displaying even white teeth. Carly hesitated, wishing that she hadn't deliberately chosen a spot at least three miles away from the town so that she'd be able to work in comparative solitude. 'Will it take long?' she asked reluctantly.

'Shouldn't think so. It rather depends on what's caught round the prop. Good, you'll help, then,' he said taking her question as an affirmative. 'Let's get on board.' He stepped easily back on to the boat, expecting Carly to follow him, but turned when she stood hesitating on the bank. 'Oh, sorry.' He held out his hand to help her on board.

Carly's hand was lost in his big one. She lifted one foot in a pretty high-heeled sandal on to the deck and was pulled effortlessly up. Taken by surprise, she stumbled a little, but the man caught her, holding her for a few seconds against him. Carly's breath caught in her throat, she suddenly had the stupid feeling that she was in the grip of some twentieth-century Viking.

'Easy there! Those shoes are useless on a boat,' he observed disparagingly, looking at her sandals.

'If I'd known I would have put on a pair of Wellington boots,' Carly answered sarcastically.

He grinned, not at all put out. 'Wait here, I'll get the tools.'

He returned a few minutes later, carrying a big metal toolbox, the sort that opened out from the middle to display everything inside. He had also changed into a pair of brief red bathing trunks. Carly gulped and hastily looked away. If he'd seemed like a giant before, he looked even more like one now.

But he appeared to be quite unperturbed. Opening out the toolbox, he said, 'I'll have a look first and then tell you which tools I'll need.'

Carly didn't know what he was going to do, but she certainly hadn't expected him to step up on to the side of the boat and just jump into the river. He pulled himself round to the back of the boat, took a deep breath and dived under the water. Carly watched anxiously; no great swimmer herself, she was sure he would drown, but his head, his hair darkened by the water, soon broke the surface.

'It's worse than I thought,' he told her when he had got his breath back. 'I've picked up a bunch of barbed wire. I'll need the wire cutters.'

Carly stood in the bottom of the boat and peered down at him; it looked a long way to where he had lifted an arm towards her. 'Er—which are the wire cutters?'

'They're like a big pair of scissors but without holes for your fingers.'

At the third try Carly found the correct tool and leaned over to hand it to him, but she couldn't reach.

'You'll have to get a box or something to stand on,' the giant instructed her as if she was a midget.

Ducking her head, she went down the steps into the shadowed interior of the boat. It looked very neatly fitted out; she would have liked to look round, but there had been a peremptory note in the giant's voice. Finding a stool, she carried it outside, but before she stood on it, she carefully removed her engagement ring from her left hand and put it safely on a shelf inside the cabin, afraid of losing it in the water. Then she stood on the stool and leaned over, clinging to the side of the boat to stop herself from overbalancing.

It took quite a time to free the propeller. The man cut off bits of barbed wire and handed them up to her. Carly reached down to gingerly take them from him and went to throw them back in the middle of the river, but he shouted at her, 'Don't do that, you idiot! They'll only get caught on someone else's prop. Throw them in the bottom of the boat and I'll get rid of them later.'

'Are you going to be much longer?' Carly demanded indignantly; she felt a fool perched on the stool and every time she took something from him the giant managed to splash water on her.

'No, not long.' He dived under again and came up with a long strand of twisted wire. 'That's the last.' He passed it to her and she dropped it behind her. 'If you'll take the wire cutters, then I'll come back on board.'

Carly leaned over the side, reaching down with her right hand and automatically lifting one foot behind her to balance herself. Something caught on her tights, pricked her leg as sharply as a wasp sting and began to rake down her shin. 'Ow!' She gave a startled yell of pain, tried to jerk her leg away and keep her balance at the same time, dropping the wire cutters almost on the giant's head. The stool wobbled as she clung to the side of the boat, desperately trying to regain her balance, but then it toppled over and so did Carly, headfirst into the river.

She came to the surface, coughing and spluttering, her arms flailing in a mad panic.

'Okay, I've got you.' A hand came round her waist and held her securely, her head out of the water.

Carly turned and saw the giant's head only a few inches away. 'Get me out of here!' she screamed at him. 'Get me out!'

'All right—don't panic.' He reached down and she felt her right foot being lifted and placed on something that protruded from the bottom of the boat, out of sight under the water. 'Put your weight on that.' Carly did so and with his help was able to reach up and get hold of the side of the boat, but it was too high out of the water for her to climb in.

'I can't get up,' she yelled down at him. 'It's too high.'

'Okay, I'll give you a hand.' The giant came round behind her, put his hands under her behind and literally shoved her upwards so that she went over the side in an undignified scramble.

Carly hauled herself to her feet, her hair hanging in rat's-tails, her clothes clinging wetly to her as the water ran off into pools around her ruined sandals. The next moment the giant heaved himself easily over the side and stood beside her, his blue eyes travelling slowly over her.

'If you say one word, just one word ...' Carly threatened through gritted teeth, as near as dammit to either losing her temper or having hysterics, or even both.

The giant's mouth tightened and she was sure he was trying not to laugh, but he said, gravely enough, 'You'd better go into the cabin and get those wet things off.'

She glared at him, ready to explode. 'And just what the hell do you think I'm going to wear in their place?'

'I expect I'll be able to find you something.' And when she didn't move, 'Look, you can't possibly go home like that. Come and dry yourself off.' Adding with a crooked grin, 'I won't eat you, you know.'

She was too angry to be afraid of being eaten, although she supposed that that was what giants were supposed to do; this one, however, looked as if he could quite easily hug her to death like a bear. Still dripping, she went ahead of him into the cabin. He was too big for the boat, his head almost brushed the roof and he filled the place. This first part seemed to be a kind of workroom. Carly hesitated and let him go past, following him through a further door into what was obviously his bedroom. Going to a drawer, he pulled out some clothes and several towels.

'Here, this ought to do for you, and this. The bathroom's just through there, you can have a shower if you want.' Then he picked up a towel and some of the clothes and left her to it, carefully shutting the door behind him.

Going across to the windows, Carly closed the curtains, cutting out most of the late evening light. She looked round for a light switch but couldn't find one, but there was enough to see by. Quickly she stripped off her sopping wet clothes and left them in a heap on the floor. The bathroom was much better equipped than she had expected and it was scrupulously clean. The shower was small—she couldn't imagine the giant using it—but the water was warm and there was a big bar of unscented soap and some shampoo for her hair. When she came out, wrapped in a big striped towel with another turban-fashion over her hair, she found that the lights were on and her clothes had been taken away.

Carly looked rather dubiously at the things he had left out for her. There was a pale blue shirt with long sleeves and a pair of shorts. The shorts were a joke; when she put them on they just slipped down to her hips and hung there, threatening to fall off at the slightest movement. The shirt was better, it was so big that it came down almost to her knees, like a dress. She abandoned the shorts and kept the shirt, but she needed a belt. Tentatively Carly opened a cupboard and found, as she had hoped, that it was a wardrobe containing a couple of jackets and a dark suit. There was also a striped tie which would do for a belt. She knotted it round her slim waist, unable to picture the giant in a suit and tie; he seemed far more at home in his ragged denim shorts.

Sitting down on the edge of the bunk bed, she began to rub her hair dry when there was a sharp rap on the door.

'Are you decent yet?'

'Yes, it's okay.'

The giant came in dressed, quite conservatively for him, in a pair of very faded jeans and a blue V-necked sweater. He had dried his hair so that it was back to its golden colour again, thick and curly. Carly looked at him malevolently; he seemed none the worse for his prolonged dip in the river, whereas she felt a wreck.

'What have you done with my things?' she demanded.

'Put them to dry.' His eyes ran over her approvingly, settled on her bare legs.

She tried to tuck them out of sight, but there was a built-in drawer under the bunk. 'When you've quite finished looking at my legs,' she snapped.

He grinned amiably. 'They're really something. And the rest of you is put together okay, too.'

Her voice heavy with sarcasm, Carly answered, 'Well,

thank you. Thank you so much. Coming from you that's quite a compliment, I suppose.'

But her sarcasm ran off him like sweat off a tennis player's brow. 'That's okay. It'll take a while yet for your things to dry, so why don't we have something to eat?'

'I'm not hungry,' Carly returned obstinately.

'Well, I am.' He moved to go past her, then stopped. 'Hey, is that blood on your leg?'

Looking down, she saw a trickle of blood running down her shin. 'Oh, that must be where something hurt me and made me fall in the water.'

'You didn't just overbalance, then?'

'No, I didn't,' she answered tartly. 'I'm not quite that much of a goof. Something in the boat caught on my leg.'

'Let's have a look at it.' The giant squatted down in front of her and took hold of her ankle. His hands were surprisingly gentle for a man of his size. 'I'll get some antiseptic and clean it up.'

He went out and came back a minute or so later with a comprehensive first aid box. After mopping up her leg, he put a plaster on it and leaned back on his heels to survey his handiwork. 'As good as new,' he remarked approvingly, his eyes travelling slowly up towards her face.

Carly flushed, remembering that she wasn't wearing anything under the shirt, and brought her knees primly together.

The giant grinned and stood up. 'Isn't it about time we introduced ourselves? I'm Kyle Anderson.'

So she'd been right about him being a Viking; only someone of Scandinavian descent would have the surname Anderson. 'Carly Morgan,' she returned. Then, inadequately, 'How do you do?'

Kyle nodded and said, 'If you won't have something

to eat at least come and have a hot drink with me. That water got cold after a while.'

Carly hesitated, then shrugged. 'All right.'

He led the way through a further door into what was the equivalent of a sitting-room with comfortable seats set along each side of the boat with shelves above them crammed with books, and then on into the galley area which had a sink, cooker, fridge and working surfaces on one side, but all on a smaller scale than a normal kitchen, and a dining area on the other.

'This boat seems to go on for ever,' Carly exclaimed. 'What a neat kitchen!'

'Galley,' he corrected her. 'And the boat's seventy feet long, so there's quite a lot of space.' He turned to busy himself at the cooker and soon set a mug of hot coffee in front of her. Then he took a bottle of brandy from a cupboard. 'Want a chaser to pep it up a bit?' he offered. Carly shook her head, but he had already poured a generous portion into each mug. 'Cheers.' He lifted the mug in salute. 'Thanks for coming to my rescue. But I'm sorry it ended up like it did.'

'That's all right.' She became acutely conscious that she must look a mess. 'Look, do you think you could do something for me? I left my bag and some other things on that bench I was sitting on. Would you mind fetching them?'

'Sure.'

He went out and Carly took the towel from her hair, ran her fingers through it, hoping that it looked a little better. She would have to try and get an appointment at the hairdressers first thing tomorrow; she couldn't possibly go around looking like this until her usual visit was due in three days' time.

When Kyle came back he put her bag, sketch pad

and box of pencils, etc., down on the table in front of her. 'That was everything I could find.'

'Thanks.'

'And I found out what you caught your leg on, it was a piece of barbed wire that you'd thrown down behind you on the deck.'

'Oh. Yes, I suppose it could have been,' Carly admitted, feeling a fool. 'I'm afraid I don't know much about boats,' she added defensively.

Kyle grinned. 'That's pretty obvious.' He slid into the seat opposite her, his legs so long that his knees touched hers. She hastily moved to one side. 'Are you an artist?' he asked, nodding towards her sketch pad.

'Oh, no. I'm a dress designer,' she told him, the note of pride clear in her voice.

'I'm impressed,' he said, but he didn't sound it.

Sensitive to even the slightest mockery or ridicule, Carly exclaimed heatedly, 'There's nothing funny about being a dress designer! It takes years of damned hard work before you can even begin to make any headway, and there are hundreds of other people trying to get into the market. To succeed you've got to be really good.'

'Okay, okay.' He held up his hands in mock surrender. 'I'm quite willing to take your word for it.' An amused look came into his blue eyes. 'But I don't remember saying I found it funny.'

'You may not have said it, but you certainly gave the impression that you did.'

Kyle didn't say anything, just sat watching her with a hint of laughter in his blue eyes, and Carly suddenly felt angry again. What the hell did it matter what he thought? He was just a stranger, someone of no importance in her life, whom she would never see again after tonight. And she had met that attitude before and learnt to ignore it: Andrew had taught her that, along with many other things; he would have been disappointed to hear her outburst, have expected her to behave in a more professional, adult manner. It was stupid of her to have lost her cool like that. She tried to recover her poise and dignity, but it was difficult when you were wearing only a man's shirt and your hair was a mess.

'How about you?' she countered. 'Are you on holiday, or do you live on this long boat?'

'The *Lydia* is a narrow boat,' he corrected her. 'Long boats are what the Vikings came over in.'

Carly looked at him quickly, wondering if he'd been reading her mind, but he couldn't have known that she'd likened him to one of England's ancient invaders. 'The proper name for it is a barge, isn't it?' she pointed out, not wanting him to think her completely ignorant.

He shook his head. 'No, barges were sailing boats used on big rivers like the Thames or along the coasts. These boats were made specifically to be used on the canal system, which are mostly only a few feet wide, cuts they called them. That's why the boat's so narrow.'

'And why they call them narrow boats,' Carly finished for him. Adding sarcastically, 'Thanks for the lecture, I had no idea I was so ignorant.'

Kyle wasn't at all put out. 'Most people get it wrong. Do you live in Grantston?' he asked, naming the near-by town through which the river ran.

'Yes,' she nodded. 'I have a mews flat quite near the town centre.' Again there was that faint note of pride in her voice. She had moved into the flat only three months ago and had determinedly refused all Andrew's offers to pay the rent or to have the decorating done for her, instead doing the work herself in her spare time.

Although her pride of possession would be short-lived, because she would have to move into Andrew's large house on the outskirts of town once they were married. 'Do you know the town?' she asked the giant.

'I've only been through it a couple of times. It's supposed to be very pretty, isn't it?'

'Oh, it is. Beautiful,' Carly said enthusiastically, her mind picturing the timber-framed buildings that harmonised with mellow brick and ivy-covered stone. 'And it's very peaceful. Too peaceful really; nothing much happens there.'

'A backwater?' Kyle suggested, watching her intently as her hazel eyes lit with enthusiasm.

'I suppose you could call it that. Most of the young people seem to migrate to Bristol or one of the big West Country towns. But quite a lot of them come back eventually.'

'And do you intend to go away?'

Carly shook her head. 'Not if I can avoid it, although I went to art college in Bristol, and I might have to go there, or London, for a time if my business becomes successful.'

Kyle's left eyebrow rose in surprise. 'Your business?'

It took only those two words of prompting for Carly, her face alight with eager excitement, to tell him of the small business she was just starting, designing clothes and having them made up by two dressmakers to sell to local outlets. Kyle watched her, asked a couple of questions, and while she talked got up to pour glasses of white wine from a chilled bottle, then he got out a long baguette of French bread, butter, pâté, slices of thin, lean ham, lettuce and tomatoes and set them on the table before her. Without thinking, Carly tucked into the food, her earlier reserve forgotten as she outlined her plans.

'You seem to have it all worked out to the smallest detail,' he remarked as she came to an end.

'Oh, you have to. There's no such thing as luck in business; you mustn't leave anything to chance,' Carly told him rather pompously, unconsciously quoting Andrew.

'Doesn't that rather take the fun out of it?' Kyle observed drily.

She looked at him in surprise. She had been so engrossed in her subject that for a while she had forgotten that she was talking to a stranger, and one who wore shabby clothes and lived on a boat, at that. But oddly enough, she had been able to talk to him easily and he had seemed interested in what she had to say.

'What do you mean?' she demanded. 'Surely the fun comes out of making the business a success?'

'I expect you're right,' Kyle answered equably, refilling her glass. 'I just thought that the excitement would only come when there was some sort of crisis or challenge to cope with. How long do you think it will take to get it established?'

'About two to three years.'

'And then what do you intend to do—just go on running it?'

'Well, no. I hope I might be able to open a shop of my own, and more if that's successful. Or I might be able to diversify and go into designing wallpaper with matching bedlinen and curtains, that kind of thing. It's too early to say. Andrew says we'll have to study the market in a couple of years with regard to what have been our most successful lines.'

'Andrew?' Kyle asked casually.

Carly looked across at him. The lamplight shone on her long dark hair, curly because of her ducking, and it

accentuated the hollows beneath the fine lines of her
cheekbones, enlarged her eyes in their frame of long,
dark lashes.

'He's my fiancé, Andrew Naughton,' she replied
matter-of-factly. By now she had got used to calling
him that, and it no longer brought a defensive flush to
her cheeks.

'And is he helping you with your business?'

'Oh, yes. He's been marvellous. It would have stayed as
just an ambition if it hadn't been for him. He's helped me
a great deal on the legal and practical side. He's in
business himself, you see, and has so many contacts.' She
caught Kyle's eye and added rather tartly, 'But of course
once I get going I shall handle everything myself. And my
work is the most important part of the whole thing.
Without my designs it would be impossible.' He nodded,
apparently agreeing with her, but Carly still felt that
somehow she had to defend herself.

Kyle sat back in his seat. 'So you've got your future
all mapped out: marriage to this Andrew and an
expanding business to keep you busy here in
Grantston.'

'Well, yes, I suppose so. What more could any girl
want?' she demanded with a hint of defiance.

'Nothing, I guess. I just thought you might want to
see a bit more of the world before you settle down. Or
have you already done that?'

'Well, no. I only left college a year ago and then I
went to a textile manufacturers in Bristol for several
months to learn all the processes involved. There
really hasn't been time to travel, but Andrew has
promised that we'll go abroad often for holidays, of
course.'

'The two-week tourist bit?' Now there was no
disguising the disparaging note in Kyle's voice.

'So what's wrong with that?' Carly demanded. Belatedly she realised that she had become loquacious.

'Nothing at all.' He paused. 'But I should have thought it would be helpful to you in your work to study the fabrics and costumes of other countries.'

'It would, of course,' Carly admitted. 'But that would take time, and anyway, there are always books that you can get the information from.'

The giant's mouth twisted in amusement. 'And you have so little time left.'

Carly's chin came up haughtily for a moment, but then she gave a reluctant grin. 'Okay, that must sound pretty silly. But I'm twenty-one years old and I've been studying all that time. I feel that all my life I've been learning, learning, learning. And now I'm impatient to go ahead and *do* something, put all the knowledge to some use.'

Kyle shared the last of the wine between their glasses. 'Work and learning can be combined, you know.'

'In some careers, yes,' Carly agreed impatiently. 'But not mine. I want to really get down to creating something. To have some tangible result for all the years of study. To be successful.'

'And what happens when you get married? Will you go on with your business?'

'Oh, yes. Andrew wants me to have an outside interest. That's why he's encouraging me to start.'

'And what happens when the kids come along? Do you hand them over to a nanny or an au pair?'

Carly had lifted her glass to her mouth. She took a drink and then set the glass down on the table. 'Would you look to see if my clothes are dry yet, please?'

'Why?'

'It's getting late; I must be going.'

'Why don't you want to answer my question?'

Her hazel eyes flashed. 'Because it's an extremely personal one, of course.'

'I'm sorry if I touched you on a raw spot,' Kyle said softly.

'You didn't touch a raw spot. Not at all. It's just that I ...' Carly came to a precipitate stop, aware that she was being goaded and that Kyle was watching her keenly from apparently casual eyes. 'What the hell have my plans got to do with you?' she demanded angrily. 'And what about you, anyway? What do you do?'

Kyle shrugged and grinned. 'Nothing much. I just bum around on the boat.'

'You live on it, then?'

'Most of the time. I move around quite a bit. This summer I thought I'd explore the rivers and canals of the West Country.'

Unable to imagine such a nomadic existence, Carly said impulsively, 'But how do you earn your living? Or do you exist on unemployment benefits?' she asked disdainfully.

'Now there's a personal question,' the giant remarked, and Carly flushed, acknowledging a hit. 'No, I get work from time to time.'

'It sounds a very idle kind of life.'

'Oh, it is. Very.'

She looked at him, puzzled by the hint of amused mockery in his tone. 'But don't you want to *do* anything with your life?'

'I am doing something. I'm seeing places and enjoying myself. There's no rule that says you can only enjoy life if you're a success, you know. Especially the kind of success you mean. And I like to live at the pace life was supposed to be lived.'

'That's just an excuse,' Carly said scornfully. 'Why, you're just—just a drop-out.'

Kyle looked at her quickly and then down at the table. 'And you disapprove of drop-outs, I suppose.'

She opened her mouth to say that everyone did, but changed her mind. Shrugging, she said, 'It's your life. If you want to waste it that's up to you, really. But doesn't your family object?'

'I haven't got any family to object. I'm just a poor little orphan.'

Carly chuckled; there was nothing in the least small about Kyle Anderson. Impulsively she asked, 'But don't you get awfully lonely?'

He paused to consider the question. 'Not really. I don't get bored with my own company, if that's what you mean. And if I feel like communing with my fellow man I can always tie up at a pub or walk to one in the nearest village.'

'Yes, I suppose it's different for a man—even nowadays,' Carly mused. 'If a girl was lonely she couldn't just walk into a pub by herself.'

'Have you ever tried it?'

She shook her head decisively. 'No. We went to pubs in Bristol a few times while I was at college there, but then it was always in a crowd. And Andrew never takes me to pubs—unless they have a good restaurant there, of course.'

'Ah, yes, Andrew—I was forgetting him.'

Looking up, Carly's eyes met his and held, but then she looked down at the table, drawing an abstract pattern with one long, painted fingernail. Answering his unspoken question, she said slowly, 'Andrew is very good to me. He's a patient, kind man. I've known him a long time.' She paused, watching her finger tracing the patterns, but Kyle didn't speak. After a few moments, she added defiantly, 'And I love him very much, of course.'

'Is he much older than you?'

The unexpectedness of the question brought her eyes, wide and a little vulnerable, up to his. 'Why do you ask that?'

'Because most girls wouldn't describe the man they're going to marry as patient and kind. Somehow I think they'd prefer other attributes.'

Annoyed, Carly retorted, 'Huh, a fat lot you know about it! Why, I bet you're the type of man who has a girl in every port, or whatever.'

Kyle gave a shout of laughter. 'Seeing that I only travel about twenty miles a day, that makes an awful lot of ports!'

Carly gave a reluctant smile in return, thinking that it would take an awful lot of man to have so many girls. But then the Viking was an awful lot of man. 'Sorry, but you put my back up.'

'Have another drink,' Kyle offered, reaching one long arm across the gangway to take another bottle of wine from the fridge.

'Oh, no, I mustn't; I have to drive home.'

'You have a car?'

'Yes, a Mini. I left it in a lay-by on the main road.'

'Did your parents give it to you?'

'No, I haven't any parents. As a matter of fact Andrew gave it to me as an engagement present,' she told him, on the defensive again.

'Oh, yes; you were telling me about Andrew.'

Carly rather thought that she'd been trying to avoid that subject, although there was no reason why she should, of course; she was very proud to be engaged to Andrew. 'Well, he is a bit older than me, but that's not because he's been divorced or anything; he's still a bachelor.'

'And a bit set in his ways.'

Startled, Carly said, 'No, of course he isn't. Why should you think that?'

'Because he doesn't want any kids.'

'I didn't say that,' she pointed out tartly.

'You didn't have to.'

Her finger started tracing patterns again. 'Well, it's true that having children doesn't come into our plans for the future, but what of that? Lots of couples decide not to have children nowadays. After all, it's not exactly a very good world to bring children into, now is it?' she demanded forcefully.

The giant raised an eyebrow. 'I think it's a wonderful world,' he observed.

Carly gazed at him for a long moment and felt impelled to say stubbornly, 'I'm extremely happy.'

'Well, of course you are. Anyone can see that.' Kyle opened the bottle of wine. 'It makes a pleasant change to meet someone who's unreservedly happy. Sure you won't have some of this?' he offered, holding up the bottle.

'Just half a glass, then I really must go. You haven't been to see whether my clothes are dry yet,' she reminded him, trying to decide whether or not he was taking the mickey out of her.

'I'll look in a minute. What do you do for entertainment around here?'

'Well, there's a cinema club at the Civic Hall two nights a week, and sometimes they have plays and dances there, too. Then there are lots of pubs and several restaurants. Oh, and there's a disco in a converted warehouse every Saturday night.'

'But you don't go to that?'

'No.' Carly laughed at the thought of Andrew at a disco. 'It's hardly Andrew's thing. We mostly go out for meals, either at a restaurant or to some of his friends.

Or else we drive in to Bristol to the theatre or a concert.' She wrinkled her nose. 'It doesn't sound very exciting unless you've got a car to get about in, I'm afraid.' A thought occurred to her. 'You weren't planning on staying here, were you?'

Kyle shrugged. 'I might hang around for a couple of days or so. I'd like to explore the area.'

'How? By bus?'

'Oh, I can do a bit better than that. I have a small motorbike tied on to the other end of the boat.'

'You can see everything that's of interest in Grantston in a couple of hours.' Carly told him uneasily, suddenly not wanting him to stay around. 'Surely you'd do better to move on to a bigger town, Bristol or somewhere. You can get to the River Severn from here, you know.'

'Yes, I know. But I think I'll rest up for a while,' he answered casually.

After a moment Carly glanced down at her watch, but it must have stopped when she fell in the water, and there was no clock in the galley. 'What *is* the time? It must be getting late.' She pulled the curtain covering the window beside her to one side, but it was pitch dark, the moon obscured by a cloud.

Kyle stood up. 'There should be a watch around here somewhere. Time isn't all that important on a boat.' Going over to a drawer, he fished around in it, his back to her. 'It's nearly midnight,' he told her, finding his watch.

Carly's eyes widened in surprise; she'd no idea it was so late. 'Then I really *must* go.'

'Got to make an early start in the morning?'

'Quite early. Andrew's taking me into Bristol to shop ... to get something,' she amended, feeling somehow that she couldn't tell Kyle that Andrew was going with her to shop for her trousseau; he liked to help her choose her clothes, those that she didn't design and have made up for herself, and anyway he had insisted on paying, saying that as his wife she would have a position to keep up in the town and would need really good outfits.

'I'll see if your things are ready, then.'

Kyle went away and Carly sat listening to the sounds of the boat; the water constantly lapping against the hull, the cry of a night bird, the slight creaking of the ropes that tethered it to the bank. She hadn't noticed it before, but now she became aware of the small but constant movement of the boat as it rocked very gently in the water. They were peaceful sounds, quite different from those she was used to.

'Your bra and pants are dry,' Kyle informed her when he came back, 'but the others are still damp, especially your skirt; I don't think you'd better put that back on.'

'Then I'll have to go home in your shirt. Are my sandals okay? Oh, good,' she said when he handed them to her. 'At least I won't have to borrow a pair of your shoes.'

They both looked at each other's feet and laughed.

'I'll leave you to change. Shout when you're ready.'

Carly wriggled into her pants and put on her sandals; there didn't seem to be much point in bothering with the bra when she'd been sitting there without one all evening. She called to Kyle and he came back carrying a casual jacket and a big torch.

'Here, you might as well put this on in case it's chilly outside.' He bundled the rest of her belongings into a plastic bag while Carly put on his jacket. It was miles too big for her, her arms disappeared completely inside the sleeves and it came down below her hips.

'Just how tall are you?' she demanded.

He grinned. 'About six-three.'

'And I thought I was tall!'

She followed him out on to the deck through the door from the galley in the front end of the boat, and he helped her to step ashore, switching on his torch to light the way.

'I'll walk you back to your car. Which way is it?'

'Along the towpath for a bit and then there's a path across a field.'

They walked along together, Kyle lighting the way, although the moon had come out again and it wasn't so dark. The night was very still, especially when they started across the field and left the sound of the river behind. Carly couldn't remember the last time she'd walked through the countryside at night, couldn't remember ever having done it before, if it came to that. She was very aware of the giant striding along beside her, but not at all afraid; if he'd wanted to make a pass at her he would have done so hours ago, back on the boat. They didn't talk, the night was too still and peaceful to break it with the sound of human voices. Once she stumbled over a rut and Kyle swiftly put a hand under her elbow to steady her, then kept it there until they reached the gate at the end of the path. It was the kind of gate that kept animals from straying, what they call a kissing gate. Kyle went through first and turned back to push the gate for her, the moonlight illuminating his strong face, making him look even more like the Viking she saw him as in her imagination. She could picture him in a twin-horned helmet, a sword in his hands, ready to rape and pillage. He leaned forward and Carly's heart skipped a beat as she thought that he was going to take advantage of the age-old custom and kiss her, but he merely leant down to take

the bag from her so that she could get through more
easily.

The car was just as she'd left it. Carly unlocked it and
tossed the bag on to the passenger seat. 'What about
your shirt? How shall I get it back to you?' she asked,
giving him his jacket.

'Just look for me on the river.'

'Here?' she said uncertainly.

'Either here or nearer to the town.'

'How long for?'

He shrugged. 'As long as it takes.'

She looked at him, then got into the car, wondering
what that meant, if anything at all. Winding down
the window, she looked out and said, 'Goodnight. See
you.'

He lifted a hand in acknowledgment and stood aside.
Carly started the car and turned it round, the peace of
the night instantly broken by the noise of the engine.
She drove off up the dark road back to town and
glanced in her mirror to see the giant standing tall and
golden in the moonlight, watching her go.

The boat wasn't locked. He hadn't come when she'd
banged on the side, so Carly pushed open the door and
looked at the shelf where she had left her ring the night
before. It was empty. Her heart froze for a minute, but
then she walked through the boat till she came to the
bedroom section. Kyle was lying in the bunk fast
asleep, one bare arm out of the sleeping bag across his
chest. Indignantly Carly pulled back the curtains, letting
the morning sunlight pour into the cabin.

'Hey! Hey, wake up!' Putting her hand on his
shoulder, she shook him vigorously.

He stirred, opened his eyes and caught hold of her
wrist. His eyes seemed even bluer in the daylight.

'Hallo,' he said conversationally, apparently not at all surprised to have a woman walk in and wake him.

'My ring, where is it? It's not on the shelf where I left it.'

'No, I found it after you'd gone and put it away in the day cabin.'

'Whereabouts?' she demanded impatiently. 'Come and get it for me, Kyle. Andrew's coming to pick me up in half an hour and I must have it. I can't possibly tell him that I've mislaid it.'

He sat up. 'Well, I'm very willing to oblige you, but I feel I ought perhaps to mention that I don't bother with pyjamas.'

'What?' For a second she didn't take it in. 'Oh, really!' She marched through into the day cabin and looked round for the ring, but couldn't see it. In a couple of minutes Kyle ambled in wearing his usual pair of ragged shorts. 'Where is it? Do hurry up!'

Going over to a set of built-in drawers, he opened one and turned back to her, the ring on the end of his little finger. 'This what you're looking for?'

'Of course it is.' She took it from him and pushed the diamond solitaire on to the third finger of her left hand. 'Thanks, I've got to run now. Oh, here's your shirt, by the way.' She dropped it on to a seat as she hurried to the doorway.

'Carly!' Kyle called after her as she jumped from the boat on to the bank.

'Yes?' She turned back impatiently to see him standing in the cockpit, leaning negligently with his arms folded on the tiller.

'Did it ever occur to you that a girl who forgets her engagement ring can't be that much in love with her fiancé?'

Carly gazed at him speechlessly for a moment, then turned and ran back towards her car.

CHAPTER TWO

THE day was a hectic one; not only did they shop for her trousseau at the most exclusive shops in Bristol, but Andrew encouraged her to choose a really beautiful set of leather suitcases which would have her new initials monogrammed on to them in time for the wedding. Then she went to have a first fitting for her wedding dress, which she had designed herself, while Andrew went to his tailors, afterwards meeting up for lunch at a restaurant.

The maître d' knew them well by now and himself escorted them to their favourite table, or at least to Andrew's favourite table and now Carly's by association.

'How did it go?' Andrew asked her after they'd ordered.

'Oh, fine. It's going to look beautiful. But Andrew, all that lace—it must be going to cost a small fortune!'

He put out a hand to cover hers. 'Forget it. I told you, I want you to have a wedding to remember, regardless of cost.'

'But to wear it only once; it seems such a shame.'

'There used to be a tradition that the bride put on her wedding dress again on every anniversary, but that seems to have died out now. But perhaps you can have it made into an evening dress,' he said encouragingly.

'Perhaps. Although it seems an equal shame to spoil it.'

He smiled at her indulgently. 'Just seeing you in it

will more than cover the cost. Now forget about it; it's just part of my wedding present to you.'

'You're too good to me, Andrew.' Impulsively she leaned over and kissed him on the cheek.

'Nonsense.' He said it brusquely, but Carly knew that he liked her to show him affection in public—within reason, of course, and he proved it by immediately smiling at her and holding her hand under the table. 'How did you amuse yourself yesterday evening?' he asked her. 'I see you've done your hair differently.'

Carly laughed. 'You don't have to be so tactful, Andrew. I know it looks a mess. It got wet and I had to wash it myself.'

'Did it rain last night, then? I wouldn't have noticed at my meeting.'

'Well, no.' Reluctantly she said, 'It was the silliest thing. I went down to sit by the river and work on some new ideas and there was a boat that had broken down. I helped to pull it into the bank and managed to get wet in the process.' Somehow she didn't feel like admitting to Andrew that she'd actually fallen in.

'A local boat? Anyone we know?' Andrew had quite a few friends in the local cruising club, with whom he'd often gone out for short trips, and he was toying with the idea of buying a boat himself.

'No, it was a stranger. It was a narrow boat, not a cruiser.'

'Oh, one of those.' Andrew spoke with all the condescension of a seagoing man to a landlubber.

Carly smiled at him affectionately. Although she wouldn't admit it, especially to herself, she had lied to Kyle about Andrew. For a start he was a good deal older than she was: forty-three to her twenty-one, and she wasn't really in love with him, although she was overwhelmingly grateful and very fond of him, and she

had convinced herself that this was love, mostly because
that was what Andrew so desperately wanted her to
feel. Andrew had inherited money from his father but
was a very successful businessman in his own right, a
big fish in the small pool of Grantston. To anyone who
didn't know the circumstances it appeared that she was
marrying Andrew for his money and he was marrying
her for very obvious reasons. But it wasn't like that.
Carly's mother had died when she was very young,
leaving her, an only child, to be brought up by her
father, who worked for Andrew in the drawing office of
one of his factories. But then, a few years later, her
father had been killed in an unfortunate accident in the
firm's car park, when he had been knocked down by
another employee who had backed into him.

Although it certainly wasn't his responsibility,
Andrew had immediately taken Carly under his wing so
that she hadn't had to be put in an orphanage or
farmed out to foster-parents. He had paid for her to go
to a good school and arranged pleasant places for her
to stay in the holidays, and every Christmas she had
gone to stay with him and his mother at his big
Victorian house, The Elms, on the outskirts of
Grantston. So she had been a part of his life for over
ten years and was used to having him advise and guide
her. But it had only been since she had left school,
during the last two or three years, that she had begun to
realise that he was interested in her as something more
than just a child he had unofficially adopted. It had
been very gradual. He had been wise enough not to
rush or push her in any way, but had just let her know
by small things that he was very fond of her and
thought of her as a woman now. So the first time he
had kissed her in more than an avuncular way it had
seemed quite natural and not at all repugnant.

But then there was nothing about Andrew that could possibly make anyone feel repugnant. He was a little taller than she was, about five feet ten, with dark hair that had started to go grey at the sides and she had a suspicion he tried to darken. He kept himself fit by swimming and playing tennis, and was always well dressed and scrupulously clean; she had never seen him with dirty hands or fingernails, even when he'd been tinkering with the engine of his Jaguar, which he sometimes did. He was a good conversationalist, never lost his temper, even when provoked, and was well liked by his many friends in the town. He was also an Alderman and was in line to be Mayor, but Carly had an idea that he had turned down that honour until she agreed to marry him. He would, she knew, be proud to have her as his Mayoress.

His courtship of her had been a quiet one, so that it was only after their engagement had been announced that she found that other people regarded it in a more cynical light. She had had some remarks made to her that she found very hurtful and put her on the defensive. Andrew, when she told him, had wisely advised her to ignore it, but she noticed that the people who had made the remarks were immediately dropped from their acquaintance. But it had made her see the marriage as others might and for a little while she had been doubtful, although she hadn't said anything to Andrew. He knew her well though and, guessing her feelings, had suggested her own business, giving her something else to think about and pushing their engagement into the background for a few months, so that when he eventually asked her to set a date for the wedding Carly was quite happy to do so.

And now August the tenth was only two months away. The large and ancient parish church had been booked for the service and the Country Club for the stag party. There were to be two bridesmaids and two pages, relations of Andrew's. Two hundred invitations had been printed and were waiting for her to fill them in from the guest list that Andrew had drawn up, with the few additions of friends that Carly had made at school and college. Looking at the guest list, Carly chuckled a little; Andrew had said that he wanted it to be a day for her to remember, but she rather thought that he wanted the whole town to remember it as well. Not that she minded; if that was what he wanted then she would willingly give it to him, even though she would have been just as happy with a quiet wedding, but she owed him so much she felt that nothing she could do would ever really repay him.

They spent the early afternoon shopping in Bristol for personal things; there was no need to buy anything for the house because it was already equipped with everything, although Andrew had said that she could change anything there she didn't like. It would have been fun to start at the beginning and work out colour schemes and shop for matching towels and curtains, etc., but The Elms had been in Andrew's family for generations and there was no way she was going to persuade him to move into something smaller or more modern. Either Andrew or his mother. Because she had had to accept Mrs Naughton along with Andrew. And she had been quite happy to do so; she had always got on well with the older woman, who had been kind to her as a child. And Mrs Naughton had announced that she intended to take a cruise and make a long visit to relations in New Zealand and South Africa when they returned from their honeymoon, which was a tactful way of giving them a chance to learn to live together before she took up permanent residence again.

They drove home ahead of the rush hour traffic and Andrew dropped her off at the hairdresser's. 'Sure you don't want to have dinner at the Club tonight?' he asked her.

'No, thanks. You go ahead and have your round of golf and eat with your friends. I'll see you tomorrow evening. I want to get on with those sketches I was working on.'

'All right, darling.' He kissed her lightly; Andrew wasn't the type to show any emotion in public. 'I'll call for you at seven tomorrow. 'Bye.'

After she had had her hair done, Carly did a little shopping and walked the short distance back to her flat. It was set in a quiet row of mews flats that had once been the carriage houses and stables for the large houses in the High Street that had now mostly been converted into shops and banks, but the mews had retained its character despite changing its use. The road was still cobbled and the original ornate copper lampposts still graced it. Most of the residents had window boxes or hanging baskets of flowers to take the place of gardens, and there were tubs with laurel bushes by some of the brightly painted front doors, and here and there climbing roses growing up the walls. Some people had spoiled it a little by putting in bow windows and ornate front doors instead of leaving the originals, and Carly knew that the overall effect was rather selfconsciously pretty, but she liked it all the same and had been overjoyed when one of the houses had been converted into two flats and she had been able to get the tenancy of the upper one.

She walked down the mews carrying her bag of shopping, watching where she put her feet because of her high heels on the cobbles. Cars weren't allowed down here and a wooden seat had been put in the centre of the pavement, almost outside her flat. As she approached it, someone said, 'Hi there,' and Carly looked up, expecting to see a neighbour. But it was the Viking. He sat negligently, his long legs in denim jeans stretched out in front of him, creating an obstacle for anyone who passed by. His hands were stuck in his pockets and his pale blue shirt was open almost to the waist. Kyle got to his feet, picking up a bag from the ground beside him as he did so, and towered over her. She'd forgotten how big he was. 'We didn't finish that bottle of wine we opened last night,' he informed her. 'So I thought we might as well drink it with dinner tonight. At your place this time,' he added with a grin.

Carly stared at him, not knowing how to handle the situation. 'How did you know where I lived?'

'Looked you up in the phone book,' he replied laconically. Carly stood looking up at him until he said, 'Aren't you going to ask me in?'

She blinked and came back to earth. 'What? Oh, yes, of course.' She put down her shopping to search in her handbag for her key, aware as she did so that there were a couple of her neighbours watching interestedly farther down the mews.

Her front door opened straight into a flight of stairs going up to a small landing where there was another door opening into the sitting room of the flat. The bedroom, kitchen and bathroom all opened off this main room. Kyle picked up her shopping before she could do so and followed her up, looking round with interest. Carly had furnished the flat mostly with pieces she had bought from local house sales, and the settee and easy chairs she had recovered herself in pretty country chintz. The furniture she had stripped down to its natural wood to reveal old pine, or had repainted again in a soft green, and there was a dark green carpet on the floor that she had got in a warehouse sale. The curtains she had tie-dyed in a colour matching the carpet. At first she hadn't been going to have any chairs, just big cushions scattered on the floor, but, although he hadn't said anything, Carly had realised that Andrew didn't go much on that, so she had sold the cushions and bought the settee and chairs instead.

Kyle finished looking slowly round the room and then turned back to her, his blue eyes travelling over her sleekly elegant hair and clothes. He frowned. 'This room doesn't go with the way you look.'

'Nonsense, of course it does,' she answered shortly, having expected at least a compliment about her taste in décor.

'No, it doesn't. This is the room of someone who has a feeling for texture and colour, who can create something original out of what's to hand. But the way you look,' he frowned disparagingly at her dress with its slimline skirt, three-quarter-length sleeves and low back, 'is just a copy of a photo in some fashion magazine. And I liked your hair a lot better when it was curly,' he added for good measure.

'Well, really!' Carly didn't know whether to be flattered by the first part of his remark or insulted by the second. She decided to be insulted. 'I'll have you know that this dress came from a very good shop and is the latest fashion in London.'

'It's still wrong for you,' Kyle returned incorrigibly. 'You're a country girl, not a sophisticated townee. You ought to wear milkmaid colours and walk barefoot through fields of daisies.'

Carly laughed at him, quite unable to picture herself in that kind of setting. 'You're quite wrong. That isn't me at all. I like to wear fashionable clothes. And besides, Andrew likes me to look smart.'

'Ah, I was forgetting the boy-friend. Were you back in time this morning?' Kyle seated himself in an armchair.

'Yes, just. Did your engine start all right?'

'Sure. I'm moored nearer to town now, by the Crown and Anchor.' He named a pub that fronted the river on the edge of the town, and only ten minutes' walk away.

'I didn't know they let boats moor there for more than a few hours.' Carly went into the kitchen and began to unpack her shopping, feeling strangely unsettled.

'They don't usually.' Kyle came to stand in the doorway. 'But I flexed my muscles at the landlady so that she became quite overcome by my manly charms and said I could stay there as long as I liked.'

Carly raised her eyebrows. 'What did the landlord have to say about that?'

'There isn't one, she's a widow.'

'And a very lonely one, by the sound of it?' Carly remarked wryly.

'How so?'

'Well, she'd have to be—to fall for your charms, wouldn't she?'

'Oh, nasty,' Kyle said amiably. 'You couldn't wait to get back at me about your clothes, could you?'

'You shouldn't leave yourself wide open.'

They looked at each other and laughed, then Kyle came over to look at some of the tins she'd bought. 'What are we having for dinner?'

'Well, I was just going to open a couple of tins, but if I'd known you were coming I'd have bought steaks or something.' Carly didn't emphasise it, but there was a slight note of rebuke in her voice; if he'd looked her up in the phone book then he could quite easily have phoned to see if it was all right for him to come round.

Kyle had opened the cupboard doors where she kept all her groceries. 'My God, do you live on nothing but tinned stuff?' he demanded, looking at the rows of cans on the shelves.

'That's because I eat out a lot and if I buy loads of fresh food it just goes off.'

'I bet you're a lousy cook,' said Kyle, sorting through the tins.

'I can cook steaks and that kind of thing.'

'You don't call that cooking, do you? That's just heating things up. How are you going to manage when you're married? Does the boy-friend cook?'

'Andrew? Good heavens, no!' Carly was genuinely startled. 'They have a housekeeper. And when it's her day off his mother does the cooking.'

Kyle turned to look at her, a tin in his hand. 'His mother? You're marrying his mother, too?'

'Of course I'm not. As it happens his mother is an extremely nice woman.'

'But she's going to live with you?'

'Well—yes,' she admitted, then, tartly, 'Look, just shut up about Andrew, will you? He's nothing to do with you.'

For a few seconds he studied her face, then shrugged. 'Okay, I'll refrain from comment about your boy-friend if you'll stop being disapproving about my beard.'

Carly opened her eyes wide. 'I haven't said a word about your beard—if that's what it's supposed to be.'

'Ah, that proves it. I was quite sure you didn't like it.'

She smiled, finding it impossible to go on being angry with him. '*Are* you growing a beard?'

'It's just that I never bother to shave on the boat. Now, let's see what I can find to make into something edible.'

He turned back to the cupboard, pulling out tins, and

Carly watched him, thinking that Andrew would never find it too much bother to shave, no matter what the circumstances. But then she remembered how impeccably clean and tidy Kyle's boat had been and wondered. Somehow that didn't fit in with his lazy attitude.

They had a feast that Kyle cooked, mixing contents of tins and creating a meal that Carly could never have dreamed up in a thousand years. She helped him, watching as he worked, asking questions and handing him pans or ingredients as he needed them. They drank the wine that had been left and a lot more besides and finished the meal with a delicious pineapple pavlova.

Carly sat back, absolutely replete. 'My God, that was fantastic! Where on earth did you learn to cook like that?'

'I taught myself, out of cookery books.'

'How come?'

He shrugged. 'I lived alone and got fed up with living out of tins. So would you if you didn't have the boy-friend to keep taking you out and treating you to lavish meals.'

'I wish you wouldn't keep calling him the boy-friend,' Carly snapped waspishly.

Kyle looked at her steadily across the table. 'Sorry.'

Biting her lip, she looked away, wishing that she'd kept quiet. 'Let's listen to some music, shall we?'

'Right.' He helped her to clear away and then they put on some cassettes, Kyle sprawled out on the settee which was much too small for him, Carly on the floor, leaning back against a chair. When the cassette ended Kyle started talking and they had a heated discussion, closely verging on an argument, on the merits of different kinds of music. It wasn't the first argument they'd had that evening; over dinner they had wrangled long and happily over a variety of subjects, one seeming to lead effortlessly on to another. And Carly enjoyed it immensely; she hadn't been involved in any kind of stimulating debate since she'd left college. Andrew never argued with her on things they could do nothing about, like state education, disarmament, or politics, he merely smiled at her tolerantly when she got started and was ready to change the subject when her argument petered out in the face of his polite indifference. He would listen to her on day-to-day things, though, especially about the business, and would patiently go through things and point out to her where she was making a mistake and what it could lead to, so that she would know in the future.

It was late before Kyle left. The time had just flown and Carly was amazed when she looked at her watch and saw that it was gone one. She escorted him to the front door and they stood together for a while looking up at the clear, starlit sky. It was a very warm night, they were in the middle of one of those mini-heatwaves that sometimes hit England in June and transformed it into an Eden of rich, green loveliness. The town was quiet now, it was some distance from any motorways, so there wasn't even the hum of traffic to disturb the stillness. The street lamps had been turned off at midnight and there was only the moon to light his way.

'Don't fall in the river,' Carly warned. 'Shall I get you a torch? I think I've got one somewhere.'

'No, that's all right. Your eyes soon get accustomed to the dark.' He turned to look at her, his shadow long and dark across the cobbles. 'Come out on the boat with me tomorrow.'

She shook her head. 'I can't; I have to work on those sketches tomorrow.'

'Bring your work with you. We'll tie up somewhere

quiet, have a picnic, and I'll leave you in peace to work while I potter on the boat.'

Again Carly shook her head, but regretfully. It would be nice to get out of the flat and on to the river in this lovely weather. But you had to have self-discipline if you were going to run a business. That was one of the first things Andrew had taught her; you couldn't take time off whenever you felt like it just because you were the boss. And not only that, perhaps it would be best not to see Kyle any more. He was just a passing stranger, and although he was fun to be with, he would soon be gone, have moved on to another town and would quickly forget her. 'Thanks, but I can't make it.'

'Coward,' he goaded softly.

Carly's chin came up. 'Not everyone wants to live the kind of life you do, Kyle. You're the one who's a coward. You won't even accept the responsibility for your own future.'

'No more do you,' Kyle returned shortly. 'And at least I don't lie to myself.'

'What do you mean?' she demanded hotly.

'You're only kidding yourself with that business of yours. You've handed your whole future over to your fiancé, lock, stock and barrel.'

'That's utter rubbish! Do you think I don't have a choice in what I do?'

'Then exercise it. Come out with me tomorrow,' he challenged.

'All right, damn you, I will!'

'Good.' He grinned at her in the darkness and Carly realised she'd been outmanoeuvred.

She smiled reluctantly in return. 'I really oughtn't to, Kyle, I have so much to do.'

'I told you, you can quite easily do your work on the boat. I'll come for you about ten, okay?'

'No,' she objected quickly. 'I'll come down to the boat. By the Crown and Anchor, you said?'

'Yes. Goodnight, then. Thanks for dinner.'

'I've an idea I ought to thank you for that, after all you cooked it.'

He smiled and moved closer to her, lifting a hand to gently raise her chin. 'See you tomorrow.'

'Yes.'

He continued to gaze down at her for a long moment, then gave an abrupt nod and turned away, walking briskly but quietly down the mews. Carly watched him go, then slowly went back inside. It was late and she was tired after a busy day, but she lay awake for some time, already regretting her hasty acceptance of his challenge. What if Andrew called her tomorrow and she wasn't there? How was she going to explain where she'd been? She'd never once lied to him and she certainly didn't intend to start now. He gave her a great deal of freedom to see her own friends, recognising that she sometimes wanted to be with her own age group, but somehow she didn't think that he'd class Kyle in that category. And he might not approve of her spending the day alone with another man, however innocently. Not that Andrew would go off at her or anything, he'd never do that, but he would definitely let her be aware of his disapproval, which would make her feel wretched for days until things were all right between them again.

Carly awoke to another beautiful day. Pushing wide the window, she looked out between the houses to where she could just see the water meadows on the outskirts of town. The river was just beyond them, hidden behind the large stone building of the parish church, its spire reaching up into the pale blue sky. The church she was to be married in. She ate her usual half a grapefruit breakfast, showered, and put on a short-

sleeved red and white blouse, a full white skirt and red
high-heeled sandals. Then she collected up all the things
she needed for the day before looking up the number
for the Crown and Anchor in the phone book and
dialling it.

When a woman's voice answered, Carly said, 'I'm
sorry to bother you, but could you please give a
message to Mr Kyle Anderson who lives on the boat
Lydia?' And going on quickly, before the woman had
time to protest, 'Would you tell him that his friend is
unable to meet him today as arranged? Thank you very
much. Goodbye.'

Then she hurried out of the flat to the near-by car
park where she kept her Mini, started up the car and
drove quickly out of the town centre to the house of
one of the women who was making up her designs
for her.

That the way she had left the flat was more like
running away, Carly was fully aware. But Kyle had
long legs and she was quite sure that he would come
round just as soon as he got her message, demanding an
explanation and calling her a coward again. And she
was, she knew it. But she had no other explanation for
him than it wasn't being fair to Andrew, and somehow
she thought Kyle would only scoff at that. But it wasn't
fair, she knew in her heart it wasn't, and she should
never have said that she'd go in the first place. And it
was much better for Kyle to get the message now, she
thought firmly. There really wasn't time or a place in
her life for a friend like him. And he was too disruptive
an influence. Why, she hadn't done a stroke of work
since the moment she'd met him!

She spent an hour or so going over her designs with
her dressmaker, then drove over to Andrew's house. It
was a pseudo-Gothic building, all gables and pointed

windows. Andrew wasn't at home, of course, but his mother was. Mrs Naughton greeted her with pleased surprise. 'Hallo, Carly. I don't usually have the pleasure of seeing you at this time of the day. I'm just going to have coffee; would you like one?'

'No, but I'd like something long and cold. I found the flat too claustrophobic today and wondered if I could come and work in your garden?'

'Why, of course you can, my dear. You don't have to ask, you know that.'

The gardens at The Elms were beautiful; the trees after which it had been named had miraculously managed to avoid the Dutch Elm disease which had so ravaged the countryside and stood, tall and majestic, overlooking the long, manicured lawn, the flower beds where there was never a weed or a dead flower to be seen, the rockeries and sunken garden, and, away on the other side of the house, the walled kitchen garden and small orchard. There was also a grass tennis court and what had once been a croquet lawn, but Andrew had turned this last into a putting green. He was toying with the idea of putting in a swimming pool but hadn't got round to it yet; Carly guessed that he was waiting until they were married and for her to show some enthusiasm for the project, but she didn't want people to think she was encouraging him to spend his money; he'd been more than generous to her, as it was.

All the money she had of her own was five thousand pounds, the proceeds of an insurance policy her father had taken out, and which she had inherited when she was twenty-one. This she had used to furnish the flat, to live on now and to start her business, which hadn't yet begun to show much of a profit. Andrew was more than willing to help her, of course, and didn't really like it when she refused, but Carly was determined to keep

herself until the wedding, although there was very little
of her capital left now.

Wandering down into the sunken garden, she sat on
a stone seat overlooking a circular pool where goldfish
swam lazily among the lily stalks. The water reminded
her of the river and Kyle. She wondered what they
would have been doing now, talking or just lying on a
bank in the sun. She pushed the mental picture
ruthlessly out of her mind and turned to thank Mrs
Naughton, who had carried their drinks out on a tray.

'Are you and Andrew going out tonight, or would
you like to join my bridge party?'

'Thanks, but we're dining with the Brentons; he's
going to offer Andrew the captaincy of the Golf Club
next year.'

Mrs Naughton laughed. 'Another of Grantston's
well-kept secrets that everyone knows! Is Andrew going
to accept?'

'Oh yes, I expect so. You probably know better than
I do.'

'He doesn't tell me everything, you know.'

'No,' Carly said shrewdly. 'But what you don't know
from Andrew you probably hear from somebody else.'
For his mother had a great many friends in the town
and was a member of nearly every organisation there
was going, sitting on the committee of most of them.

The older woman laughed. 'True. There isn't much I
don't get to know about sooner or later. I even guessed
that Andrew wanted to marry you before he knew it
himself.'

'Didn't you mind?' Carly asked curiously.

'Good heavens, no! I've been looking after him quite
long enough; it's about time some other woman took
the job off my hands and gave me some freedom.'

Carly smiled politely but wondered whether Mrs

Naughton realised she had made it sound like a jail sentence.

They talked for a little longer and then the older woman left her alone to get on with her work. She found it strangely difficult to get started, but once she did Carly became engrossed, lost to her surroundings and the time. She was working on winter clothes, trying to design a range of casual garments that were smart as well as warm, aiming to produce separates that could be worn by all age groups, not the kind of fashion-conscious clothes that were worn for a season and then junked, but well-cut things of high-quality materials that could be brought out and adapted year after year.

At one, Andrew's housekeeper called her in for lunch which she ate alone, Mrs Naughton having gone out, but her mind was on her work and she went back to it immediately. The sun slid gently behind the elm trees, leaving her in shadow, and Carly stretched her stiff limbs. It was five o'clock, time to stop work and go home. Packing her things into the Mini, Carly drove back into town, full of that satisfied feeling one gets after having worked hard at something creative. It was the rush-hour and the roads were busy with cars and bicycles, with buses stopping to pick up passengers, the pavements crowded with pedestrians. She stopped in line at some traffic lights in the wide high street that used to be a market place a century ago and waited patiently for a mob of people to cross before they turned to green. Among the crossing pedestrians one figure stood out, his fair hair golden in the sun, head and shoulders taller than nearly everyone else. Kyle crossed the road and started to walk along the opposite side. Then he glanced over and saw her.

Immediately he turned back and tried to get across the road to her side, but the lights changed and the cars started off, so he waited for a gap and then dodged between them, signalling her to wait. But Carly didn't; she just put her foot down and sped after the car in front, carefully not looking in Kyle's direction as she did so. She was more than half afraid he would follow her to the flat and expected the bell to ring all the time she was there, getting ready to go out for the evening, but fortunately it didn't. Maybe this time Kyle had really got the message.

Andrew called for her at seven and drove her in his Jaguar to the Brentons' house. George Brenton was the current Captain of the local Golf Club. Sometimes Carly found it a bit odd to call people old enough to be her parents by their Christian names, but they were near enough Andrew's contemporaries and it would have looked even odder if she'd called them Mr or Mrs. They had a very pleasant meal; the Brentons' daughter and son-in-law were also there, so Carly didn't feel at all out of place. They left at about eleven-thirty, Andrew having accepted the Captaincy after taking her aside and asking her if she minded. Of course she had told him to go ahead and do what he wanted; his asking her had really only been a token gesture, but she appreciated him making it. He drove slowly home, although he had been careful not to have too much to drink, and he was a very safe driver anyway.

'Mother said you came round to work in the garden today,' he remarked.

'Yes, it was too hot to stay indoors.'

'I'm glad you came to the house; I don't like you going in the public park or down by the river. You never know who you might meet.'

Well, that was true enough, Carly thought with an inward smile; you never knew when you might run into a fair-haired giant, a Viking to invade your peace.

'Did you get much done?' Andrew was asking her.

'Yes, loads. I was really able to concentrate.'

'Good. I was thinking; how would the idea of converting that old summerhouse into a studio appeal to you? It needs some repairwork done to it and we could convert it at the same time.'

'It sounds a marvellous idea—and very practical.'

Andrew smiled. 'I expect you think I'm too practical. But it's just my natural way of looking at things, I'm afraid.'

'Of course, I don't. You're always thinking of things to please me. You must know how grateful I am.'

He turned to smile at her and let his hand cover hers and squeeze it for a moment before returning to the steering-wheel. When they reached the mews, he left the car and walked back to her flat with her, coming upstairs to say goodnight. Carly turned on the lamps and drew the curtains, then Andrew took her in his arms and kissed her in growing passion.

'God, I wish it was August and we were married,' he said thickly, his hand on her breast.

'It won't be long,' she reminded him, drawing away a little.

'Even one day is too long.' He kissed her again, then looked at her in the dim light. 'You're tired. And I've a heavy schedule ahead of me tomorrow. I'll give you a ring about six and we'll decide how we want to spend the evening.'

'All right.' Carly went with him to the front door and watched him walk down to the end of the mews and wave before getting in his car and driving away.

It was another lovely night; you could count the stars in the sky if you had patience enough. She felt suddenly very small, very infinitesimal in the scheme of things. With a little sigh, she turned to go in, but then someone said softly, 'Carly,' and she looked round, thinking for a stupid moment that Andrew had come back. But it was Kyle. He stepped out of the deep shadow of a doorway into the moonlight and walked towards her.

'You couldn't come on the boat this morning, so how about coming tonight?' he said, his eyes fixed on her face.

She stared at him, unable to really believe that he was there. The moonlight played on him, giving a ruthless edge to the planes of his face. She could imagine how his ancestors had struck terror into the hearts of the people they had invaded. 'You mean—now?' she faltered.

'Of course now.'

'But—but that's crazy!'

'Why? Have you ever been on a river at night? That's the best time. Come on,' he urged her, reaching out for her hand.

'I can't go like this,' Carly objected, playing for time, indicating her black silk dress and high heels. 'I'll have to go and change.'

She turned to go in, but Kyle caught her arm. 'Oh, no, you don't. If you go back inside that flat you'll change your mind. So you'll have to come as you are.'

There was no time to protest. Carly had just time to pick up her bag from the little table in the hall and close the door, then she found herself being hurried along to where a motorbike was parked at the kerb.

'Here, put this on.' He handed her a crash helmet and put one over his own fair hair. It only needed a couple of horns sticking out of it to make the picture complete. Carly fumbled with the straps of the helmet and he impatiently did it up for her. Then he grinned. 'You look ridiculous.'

He got on the bike and Carly dazedly hitched up her skirt and climbed on to the pillion seat behind him.

'Hold on,' he ordered, and she obediently put her arms round his waist, holding tightly, her chest pressed against his back. The engine split the silence and then they were off, speeding through the night, the wind catching her clothes and her hair. A sudden, over-whelming surge of exhilaration filled her and Carly laughed aloud with excitement. She clung to the giant, happy to let him take her wherever he wanted to go.

CHAPTER THREE

IT was mad, that ride through the night. Carly was lost to everything but sensation; the breeze that cooled her heated body and pulled at the skirt of her dress, the noise of the engine muffled by the crash helmet, the hardness of Kyle's body between her arms, their speed, and the feeling of exhilaration mixed with fear that sent adrenalin bubbling through her veins. The ride was too short, they soon came to a track that led off the main road and down to the river. Kyle slowed down and they bumped along it until they reached the *Lydia*, moored beneath a slight bank near a group of willow trees that stretched their green fronds down to the surface of the water.

Kyle helped her off the bike, then picked it up in his strong arms and carried it down to the bank, lifting it on to the roof of the boat. 'Come on.' Carly hesitated, and he came back, swung her up into his arms and carried her on to the boat with as little effort as he would carry a bag of groceries. 'There!'

'It was only my shoes,' she protested.

'I know.' He smiled down at her. 'Go and find something of mine to wear while I secure the bike on the roof.'

She found another of his shirts, a check one this time, and used the same tie as a belt. Her shoes she just kicked off and left in the cabin with her dress, then she hurried eagerly out to find him.

He was the bank, pulling out the mooring stakes, and jumped quickly back on board before the boat could drift out. 'Stow these away in that locker, would you?' he asked, handing the stakes to her. He started the engine and the narrow boat pulled gently into the middle of the river, its engine making a soft phut-phutting noise that in no way disturbed the calm of the night. They travelled slowly, leaving only a small wake behind them that rippled across the flat surface of the river and broke gently against the banks, hardly disturbing the small creatures that lived in holes in the mud.

Carly stood beside Kyle in the cockpit, watching as he steered the boat by the long arm of the tiller. She could imagine him standing at the prow of a Viking longboat, looking out over misty seas, the blood-red sail unfurled to catch a wind to carry them to the west. But this was the peace of twentieth-century England, the moon was out, dappling the river as they passed trees and then open fields, going from utter darkness into a light almost as bright as day as it was reflected off the water. The boat lights Kyle had turned on, red on the left and green on the right, were hardly necessary, there was no other traffic on the river, although occasionally they passed a boat moored against the bank.

'Where are we?' Carly asked at length, breaking the peaceful silence.

'Don't you know?'

'No, it all looks different from the water.'

'We're a few miles outside Grantston, in the opposite direction from where you helped me the other night. Look, over there, can you see a church steeple? That's the village just before you get to Grantston.'

'Appleby,' said Carly with a nod, thinking that eventually they would be passing near Andrew's house where he would be asleep, quite unaware that she wasn't safely at home in her flat. For a brief moment she felt a stab of guilt, but pushed it to the back of her mind; tomorrow she might feel guilty, but not tonight. Tonight was time out.

As if reading her thoughts, Kyle said, 'Do you know what night it is? Midsummer Eve. And there's a new moon. In medieval times people used to believe that the period of the midsummer moon was a time of madness when people did crazy things.'

'Midsummer madness—yes, I've heard of it. So it's all right for us to be a little crazy—just until the moon dies,' Carly said, more to herself than to Kyle.

He grinned at her. 'Come and take the tiller.'

'Oh, I couldn't. I don't know how.'

'It's easy. Come on, I'll show you.'

She ducked under the tiller and stood just in front of him. He showed her how to take the wooden bar in her hand, resting her arm along the top of it, moving the tiller from side to side in small, easy movements to follow the bends of the river. They were going very slowly, not more than four miles an hour, but even so it seemed very fast to Carly as she tried to stay in the middle of the river, her tongue between her teeth as she concentrated. The only time she had been on boats before was when she had been invited along with Andrew, on his friends' big cabin cruisers. And then they had been purely social occasions; she had either sat on a comfortable seat in a roomy cockpit or down in a beautifully fitted-out cabin with the other women, leaving the men to take the boat a couple of miles down river and moor up at a pleasant spot that was often enough the boat-owner's back garden, where they would all alight for food and a great many drinks before cruising back again. There were, she knew, some boatmen who took their craft down the Severn and over to Ireland or France for their holiday, but for most of them it was just an excuse for social get-togethers.

And it was definitely a far cry from this sort of boating; gliding through the darkness with the moon to light their way, the river as soft and still as the night.

'Watch out for that log!' Kyle warned.

She pushed the tiller over, but too abruptly, and they turned into the low-hanging branches of a tree. Immediately Kyle's hand covered hers, steering them back into open water, and at the same time he pulled Carly round, holding her head against his chest, so that the branches that dragged along the boat pulled only at her hair, and didn't scratch her face or endanger her eyes. Her face was against the bare, warm column of his throat; she could smell the faint tang of piney soap, feel the throb of life in his pulse.

He let her go. 'Okay?' She nodded and took over the tiller again, but he was standing closer to her now, she could feel his body touching her shoulder and her hips, and it seemed quite natural for him to put an arm lightly round her waist as he watched to see that she came to no harm.

About half a mile further on he took over, steering into the bank and tying up to a tree where there was a clear pool of water where a shallow stream flowed into the river.

'This is a good place for a swim,' he told her. 'The water's clean and there aren't any weeds. I found it the other day.'

'You go ahead—I'll watch.'

'Aren't you coming in?'

'No, I had my hair done yesterday.'

He laughed, the sound frightening a moorhen that scuttled away along the bank. 'Oh, Carly! Is that midsummer madness, worrying about your hair?'

'Well, I haven't got a bathing suit,' she said defensively.

He shrugged. 'Who needs one? I never use one.'

'It seems to me,' Carly told him tartly, 'that you seem to manage with very few clothes on this boat.'

'I like to travel light,' he grinned at her. 'Turn your back if you're shy; I'm going in.'

She turned and studied the river bank as she heard him taking off his clothes and didn't turn around until she heard the splash he made as he dived into the water. His head broke the surface and he said, 'It's beautiful. Why don't you come in? You'll always regret it if you don't, you know.'

Carly peered over the side at him. 'How deep is it?' she asked suspiciously.

'Not very deep. Look, I'm standing on the bottom.' The water came up to his chest. Carly did a mental calculation and figured that she would be able to keep her head out.

'Haven't you got a shower cap I could use?' she asked.

'What on earth would I want with a shower cap? Come on, woman,' he ordered peremptorily. 'Don't be such a coward. You know you want to.'

'How can I get in?'

'I've put the ladder on the side; you can climb down that.' He pointed at a solid set of steps he had clamped to the side of the boat.

'All right then, but you've got to turn your back.'

Kyle laughed again. 'What will I be turned into if I peek?'

'Something really diabolical like a rat or a toad. Although you're halfway to being one of those already.' Carly slipped off her clothes. 'Okay, now turn round.' She waited until he'd done so and began to climb down the ladder. 'Ooh, it's cold!'

'It's fine once you're in completely. Just let go the ladder and drop.'

'No fear! You go in your way, I'll go in mine. And keep your back turned,' she snapped out as she thought he was going to turn round. 'I'm not in yet!' She gasped as the cold water rose up her body. The ladder came to an end and she had to let her legs drop and come down on her hands. Her feet touched the bottom and she let go the ladder, dipping her shoulders under the water so that she stopped shivering. 'Mmm, you're right—it is beautiful.'

'Is one allowed to turn round now?' Kyle demanded.

'One is. But if you try to duck or splash me I shall get straight back in the boat and I'll never speak to you again,' she warned.

'Race you across to the bank,' Kyle challenged.

'I'm not very good. You'll win easily.'

'Okay, I'll give you a pick-a-back ride. Hold on to my shoulders.'

Carly did so and he carried her along swimming powerfully while she floated on the water. Sometimes her body touched his, but there was nothing sexual about it and she felt completely natural there without any clothes. The water was beautifully cool against her hot skin and it rippled sensuously along her body as Kyle pulled her along. He reached the bank and stood up, and Carly let go of his shoulders and moved back a couple of paces so that the water covered her chest. Kyle pretended to chase her and they played silly games, but he was a much better swimmer than she and could even dive right under the boat and come up on the other side, much to Carly's astonishment when he suddenly appeared beside her. They trod water, holding hands companionably, and sang 'Ol' Man River' in the style of Al Jolson, then 'Moon River', the 'Eton

Boating Song' and all the other tunes they could
think of that had the slightest connection with water,
much to the consternation of a cow that came down
to the far bank to drink and hastily lumbered away
again.

'A very good critic, I'd say,' Kyle remarked. 'She
obviously can't stand your singing.'

'Mine?' Carly choked with indignant laughter. 'Have
you heard yourself? You sound like the proverbial tom-
cat who's burnt his feet on a hot tin roof!'

'Now that definitely calls for a ducking,' Kyle
threatened, and moved to grab her.

'No! You promised!' Carly yelled, and tried to move
away, but he caught her, grabbing her round the waist
and pulling her to him, laughing at her. But then the
laughter faded from their faces as their bodies touched
and they realised they were naked. Quickly, then, he let
her go.

'We'd better get back on the boat,' he said after a
moment. 'We'll start to get cold if we don't.'

'Must we?' Carly protested. 'It's so lovely in the
water.'

'We'd better. We must have been in here for nearly
an hour. I'll go first and get some towels.'

He climbed back on board and Carly had a glimpse
of his lean, tautly muscular body before she turned for
a last swim. She wasn't afraid of the water now, almost
felt as if it was her right element, she was enjoying it so
much. Before she had only ever paddled in the sea or
swum at public swimming baths that were full of
chlorine and people who splashed and shouted noisily,
where there were no soft waves to caress her or peace
and stillness to calm her fears. Or a man to take care of
her.

'Come on in!' Kyle called, and she swam over to the

ladder. He had tied a towel sarong-fashion round his waist and was holding another one ready for her.

Carly climbed the ladder, stepped over the side, and he wrapped the towel round her and began to rub her dry. And that, too, seemed a perfectly natural thing for him to do. When she was dry, he went below while she dressed and came back carrying two mugs of steaming hot cocoa. They sat together in the cockpit in the bow, sipping their drinks, not saying a great deal, their shoulders touching.

'I haven't done anything as crazy as this since I was in college,' Carly remarked at length.

'Mm, people tend to go a little mad during their student days,' Kyle agreed.

'How do you know? Did you go to college?' He hesitated for a fraction of a second, then nodded silently. 'Which one? What subjects did you take?'

Kyle grunted. 'It was a long time ago. Talk about something else.'

'Why, because you didn't stay the course? Or because you failed?' She looked at his alert blue eyes and intelligent face and somehow couldn't believe that he had simply failed. There had to be more to it than that. 'I don't understand you, Kyle.'

'Then don't try. Just accept me for what I am, for what you see.'

'But it's such a waste,' she burst out.

Leaning forward, he placed a long finger over her lips. 'Don't spoil it, Carly,' he said softly.

Slowly she relaxed; he was right, of course, tonight was too perfect to spoil by quarrelling. Leaning back against the bulkhead, she said, 'Where will you go from here?'

Kyle shrugged. 'I don't know. I can go anywhere I like: north to the Midlands, west into Wales, or east towards London. The country is my oyster, open for me to enjoy. If I see a canal or river that looks inviting I can turn into it. If I see a pub that advertises food and a good make of beer, then I'll stop and eat and drink.'

'And what happens when you run out of money, or the weather gets cold, or you get fed up of just wandering aimlessly? Then what do you do?'

'If I want to, then I'll take a job for a while. Like at the Crown and Anchor; I'm cleaning out the cellar and re-whitewashing the walls for the landlady in exchange for being allowed to moor there.'

'You never told me you were working there?'

'Well, I'm telling you now. There are no set times, I just do a few hours when I feel like it. Finished?' He indicated her mug of cocoa.

'Yes, thanks.' She handed him the empty mug and he took them down into the cabin, coming back dressed in jeans and a lightweight sweater. 'Will you move on when you've finished the cellar?' Carly asked him when he rejoined her.

'Possibly.' He stood looking down at her, her dark hair dishevelled, the ends still a little damp from their swim. 'Why don't you come with me?' he asked steadily.

She sat very still for a long moment, then got to her feet. 'You're joking, of course,' she answered lightly, not looking at him.

'What makes you think I'd joke about something like that?'

She turned on him in sudden anger. 'Now who's spoiling things?'

Kyle's mouth twisted into a crooked smile, but then he nodded, 'Quits, then?'

'Yes, I suppose so,' she answered in a grumbly tone, then shivered suddenly. 'I'm cold.'

'I'll get you my jacket.'

He fetched the same jacket that he had lent her before and Carly snuggled into its warmth. It smelt of Kyle, of his maleness. Untying the ropes, he started up the engine and they sailed slowly along. The moonlight had faded and for a while it was completely dark, but then the sky started to lighten and she realised with astonishment that it would soon be dawn. The time had gone so quickly, she could hardly believe it, and she didn't feel in the least tired. She glanced at Kyle and smiled a little, thinking that his Viking ancestors wouldn't have accepted her refusal so easily, they would simply have slung the reluctant wench over their shoulder and carried her down to their long boat, regardless of her screams and tears.

'Penny for them?' Kyle offered, seeing her smile.

She shook her head. 'They're not for sale.'

'Were you thinking of your fiancé?'

'Of Andrew?' There was surprise in her voice. 'Oh, no, I wasn't thinking of him.'

'Good. Maybe there's hope for you yet.'

Carly looked at him, knowing that he was trying to goad her but unwilling to argue. 'We said quits, remember?'

He was silent for a few minutes and then said, 'Why didn't you give your name to the landlady at the pub when you phoned this morning and broke our date?'

'Didn't I? I expect I forgot.'

'Don't lie, Carly. You know damn well you didn't. Was it because of Andrew? Are you afraid of him?'

'Of course not. It's just that—well, he's quite well known in the town and most people seem to know I'm engaged to him. I didn't want it to get back to him, that's all.'

'Want what to get back to him—that you were going out for a few hours with a friend?'

'It isn't that simple,' Carly answered, aware that she was on the defensive again. 'If there had been four of us, or even just another girl, it would have been fine. But we were bound to have been seen by someone who knew me, and you don't know how people gossip in a small town like this; I do,' she said feelingly.

'You've already experienced it?'

'Yes. After our engagement was announced—well, there was a lot of talk. People thought that I was marrying him for his money. And that he . . .' She broke off and waited for Kyle to comment, but when he didn't, she said sharply, 'Well? Aren't you going to ask me if I *am* marrying Andrew for his money?'

'I don't have to. I know you're not.'

'How can you possibly know?'

He shrugged. 'Call it instinct. Just as instinct tells me that, whatever your reasons for marrying him, you're not in love with him.'

'Yes, I am. Of course I am. If I wasn't in love with Andrew, or wanted his money, what other possible reason could there be for marrying him?'

'People get married for lots of other reasons: for companionship, security, or just because they don't want to be single any longer, or even out of pity, or gratitude. Which one is yours, Carly?'

'None of them. I love Andrew.' She turned her head away and looked towards the town, not far away now, across the water meadows. A large bird rose suddenly from the marshy ground, the beating of its wings loud in the stillness. As if it was a signal, the air was at once filled with the song of every bird in the area, the chorus swelling as each new species sought to dominate those that had gone before. Carly listened in fascination; she had taken birdsong as a matter of course all her life, but realised that she had never really listened before and wished she could recognise the different calls. The greyness of the dawn began to turn to gold as the sun began to rise into a sky that turned to brilliant blue, as light and clear as Kyle's eyes.

'Look,' Carly whispered, afraid of breaking the spell, 'the dawn's breaking.'

'Bliss was it in that dawn to be alive, But to be young was very heaven,' Kyle quoted softly.

Somehow it didn't seem at all strange that he should quote Wordsworth, in some ways only poetry could match that miraculous dawn, as night turned to day in a glorious blaze of red and gold.

They reached the meadow and Kyle slowed the engine even more so that it made very little noise as the *Lydia* glided through the outskirts of the sleeping town. Here there were mostly large houses with their lawns sloping down to the river, and often with big, seagoing pleasure boats moored to the bank, some of which Carly recognised as those she'd been invited on with Andrew. After the large houses there were rapidly increasing estates where the big houses had been torn down to make way for terraces of new, much smaller houses with minute gardens, sold mostly for their snob value of backing on to the river, but too close to its dampness and chill in winter. Then these gave way to the old Victorian and Edwardian warehouses that had been built when the river was in its heyday as a working waterway and boats had come from far and wide to unload their wares and load up again with the woollen cloth for which the town had once been famous. This industry had now disappeared completely and the high, mellow brick buildings had been divided into small factory units, their façades a hotch-potch of name signs and advertisements.

The Crown and Anchor was at the end of the warehouses, just before the town really got started. It was an old place that seemed to sag in the middle, with small-paned windows and a paved terrace overlooking the river.

'Get ready with the rope,' Kyle warned her, and turned off the engine as he steered into the bank.

Carly jumped off as soon as they were close enough and Kyle helped her to make the boat fast to the big old metal rings set into the concrete piling holding up the terrace, proof that boats had been tying up there for innumerable years.

Straightening up, Carly looked at him. 'It's Midsummer Day,' she said quietly, almost wistfully. 'The midsummer madness is over.'

'No, it lasts while the moon lasts, remember?' he answered in firm denial.

She smiled but shook her head a little. 'I'll go and change.' Going down into his cabin, she pulled off his jacket and stood looking down at her discarded clothes: the sophisticated black dress and high-heeled shoes. Impulsively she opened the door to his wardrobe and looked at her reflection in the mirror there, seeing the other Carly, long dark hair a little untidy, eyes aglow with the dawn, and dressed just in Kyle's check shirt, a girl gripped for a few hours by midsummer madness. But the time had come when she must go back to her old life. Cinderella in reverse, she thought with a small smile. Her fingers moved to the makeshift belt at her waist and slowly undid it, let it fall to the ground. There was a slight sound and she looked into the mirror to see Kyle duck into the cabin behind her. His eyes met hers in the mirror—and held.

He remained where he was in the doorway for a long moment, then slowly moved towards her, his eyes still holding hers. He put his hands on her shoulders and she trembled violently.

'You don't want to go back,' he said softly, his breath brushing her ear. 'Why don't you admit it, Carly?'

'No. No, that isn't true. I must go back.'

'But you don't want to. Do you? *Do you?*' His hands gripped her shoulders, then he deliberately lowered his head to gently kiss the soft, cool flesh of her neck. She felt the warmth of firm lips moving on the long tendon just behind her ear, the mouth browsing, resting.

'Kyle . . .'

'Stay still.' His voice was soft, the words said on a long sigh of pleasure—or regret.

'Don't. Please don't.' But the words came out in a whisper and she closed her eyes, tilting her head back so that he could more easily reach the long column of her neck. His lips were warm and sensuous against her skin, sending delightful tremors through her body. Carly sighed and his hands tightened for a moment, then released her shoulders and slipped beneath her arms, up to the buttons of her shirt. His fingers didn't fumble, they were sure as they undid the first two buttons. But then Carly turned within his arms, her hazel eyes gazing up into his, troubled and afraid.

Slowly Kyle lifted his right hand to cup her chin, his eyes still holding hers, and gradually the fear left her. His mouth brushed hers lightly, a touch, no more, soft yet deeply compelling. She shuddered again as his lips moved over hers, exploring, seeking, as she stood perfectly still, aware only of the touch of his mouth and the warmth of his fingers on her skin. Her eyes were closed, but she knew somehow that his were not, that he was looking into her face as he kissed her and

wanted her to do the same. But she kept her eyes tightly
shut, as closed as her mind, aware of nothing but the
sensuousness of the moment.

His arms went round her, drawing her close to him as
he kissed her unhurriedly, taking her submission as his
by right. His kiss lit small flames of need that
threatened to grow and consume her. She began to
respond, returning his kiss ardently, but only her
mouth moved under his, her body was still and her
arms stayed by her sides.

At last Kyle lifted his head and she opened her eyes,
looked up into his face. The blue eyes seemed to burn
into hers, filled with a mixture of intense desire and
triumph. Carly was suddenly afraid that he would want
to take her, here and now, but for the moment he was
content to leave it where it was and not push her any
further. He kissed her again, lingeringly, then said, 'I'll
wait for you on deck.'

As if in a dream, she changed into her own clothes,
but slowly and with a strange reluctance. She tried to
pull herself together; after all, what were a couple of
kisses? But she was still held in the thrall of the spell the
night had cast over her, still lost in the sensations his
kiss had aroused.

She put on her shoes and then straightened up,
looking round the cabin at the long, narrow bunk that
must have been specially built to take Kyle's long
length, at the shelf full of books, some paperbacks,
others on boating. There was a barometer fixed to the
bulkhead and a round mark where there had been a
matching clock which he had obviously taken down.
There weren't many things lying around, Kyle was too
tidy for that, just a map of the inland waterways system
of the area pinned to the wall together with a list of
lock opening times. Nothing personal to tell her of his

character at all. Reaching down, she ran a hand gently across his pillow, picked up his jacket and put it on, then looked round for a last time, imprinting the cabin on her memory.

Kyle was waiting for her on deck, patiently sitting in the cockpit, quite content to let her take her time. He took her hand as she came up to him, looking up into her face, that small spark of triumph still in his eyes.

'I'm ready to go,' she told him.

'Are you?'

She nodded silently, recognising the deeper meaning behind the question.

'All right.' He stood up and stepped from the boat to the pub terrace, turned to help her follow him. It must have been about five in the morning, the sun was higher in the sky now and reflected off the mullions in the window-panes of the pub.

Carly put up a hand to shield her eyes and caught a movement in one of the windows in the upper floor. Looking up beneath the shelter of her hand, she just glimpsed a woman's face peering down at them before it was quickly withdrawn. Oh hell! Presumably that was the widowed landlady.

They walked as quickly as they could through the still sleeping streets, although Carly's high heels seemed to echo noisily with every step she took. She had never been out in the town this early before, there was a fresh, expectant air about it, as if it, like the birds, was ready to welcome this bright new day. There were few people about at this time: just a man in the dark uniform and peaked cap of British Rail cycling on an aged, squeaky bicycle towards the station; a milk lorry loaded with empty churns leaving a small dairy that still distributed its own milk and cream products; some women walking to their jobs as office cleaners, and one or two cars driving home from the night shift at a local engineering firm. No one she knew. No one to make her feel so nervous of the curious looks they gave them and make her turn her head away as if she was ashamed.

As they turned into the High Street, the sun shone fully down its length giving a golden glow that reflected off shop windows and created a hazy sheen on the tarmacked surface of the road.

'The golden road to Samarkand,' Kyle observed. 'Haven't you ever wanted to see it, to travel down it?'

'I read about that in the paper recently,' Carly answered. 'It seems that now it's nothing more than a filthy dirty track in the middle of a rundown industrial area and no one goes there but rosy-eyed tourists who have all their illusions shattered.'

Laughing mockingly, Kyle said, 'Oh, Carly, how prosaic you've become! Whatever happened to midsummer madness?'

They had reached the turn-off to the mews. Carly stopped and faced him. 'It's over. It has to be. And I don't want to see you any more, Kyle. You're no good for me. You're just endangering everything I have, everything that means anything to me.'

His eyes hardened. 'How can I endanger your life if you're really in love? If you're really sure that you've got what you want?'

'I'm not going to argue about it, Kyle. If I listened to you . . .' She made a hopeless gesture. 'Tonight has been just a—oh, I don't know—a last fling or something. But it's over and I'm going to forget it now. Just like I'm going to forget you.'

'You won't forget. You couldn't. Not after the way you responded when I kissed you. You're only lying to yourself, Carly—admit it.'

'No, that isn't so. That wasn't me. It was . . .' She

shrugged helplessly. 'I don't know. I'm all mixed up. I only know that I've got to stop seeing you—*now*.' A newspaper boy on his bicycle rode by, looked her up and down and whistled cheekily. 'I must go—I feel as if I'm on exhibit at a peepshow. Goodbye, Kyle.'

She moved to hurry away, but Kyle caught her wrist. 'No, not yet. You can't just walk away and leave it. Don't you realise that you're at a crossroads in your life?' he said urgently. 'Your whole future could depend on what you decide now.'

'I've already decided; I'm happy as I am.'

'No, you're not. If you stay here you'll be like a needle stuck in the groove of a record, going on and on, year after year, never doing anything different, until the record comes to an end and you're dead,' he told her brutally. 'What have you seen? What have you done, Carly? Do you really want to be as good as dead at twenty-one?'

She glared at him angrily. 'And do you call what you do living? Well, I don't. I think you're running away from life because you're afraid to face up to its responsibilities. You're urging me to change, but I bet you wouldn't if I asked you to. Would you?' Kyle opened his mouth to reply, but before he could do so, she said, 'No, don't answer. It doesn't matter; the question doesn't arise. It's—it's over, Kyle. I don't want to get involved.'

'You already are involved, Carly, *and* you know it.'

'No.' An electric milk float, its bottles rattling, trundled by and she tried to pull her wrist free. 'Let me go, Kyle—please.' And she didn't mean just her wrist.

'Will you kiss me goodbye?'

The colour fled from her face and she stared at him, pale and dark-eyed, unable to speak.

'You see? You can't.' He suddenly let go her wrist.

'Run away now, if you must. But you'll be back. You know you'll be back.'

Carly gazed up at him and tried to deny it, but no words came out. Turning on her heel, she ran towards the safety of her flat as if all the Viking hordes of Scandinavia were after her.

CHAPTER FOUR

FOR the next couple of days, Carly lived her life through the telephone, not daring to go out in case she ran into Kyle. She was quite certain that he hadn't left the town and often went to look cautiously out of the windows that overlooked the mews to see if he was outside, waiting for her to come out as he had waited before. In her determination to be finished with him she had forgotten to give him back his jacket and she was afraid he would use that as an excuse to call, but he didn't. She found it very difficult to concentrate on her work, a thing that had never happened to her before, her thoughts wandering so that she gazed blindly down at the sketch on her work table. Once she even came back to reality to see that she'd drawn pictures of a narrow boat all along the bottom of a design. Angrily she tore it up and hurled it into the waste-paper basket, furious with herself for having so little willpower.

On the second evening, Andrew came to pick her up and take her to the birthday party of one of his business friends who was also to be an usher at their wedding. The friend, Clive Moresby, had been married for years and lived in a detached house on a new estate in a neighbouring town. Carly knew him and his wife, Anne, quite well as Andrew had invited them over for dinner at The Elms a couple of times and they were also members of the Golf Club, but she had never been to their house and met their family before.

There were already quite a number of guests at the house when they arrived, most of them strangers. Anne

71

started to introduce them to a few people, but then some more guests arrived and she had to leave them on their own.

'I'll go and get some drinks,' Andrew volunteered.

He went off to the kitchen which was being used as a makeshift bar, and Carly moved over to the big patio windows, almost as wide as the sitting-room, and stood looking out into the garden.

'Hallo. I don't think we've met.' Carly turned as a young man about her own age with curly brown hair and a pleasant grin came up to her. 'I'm Jon Moresby.'

'Carly Morgan. You're Clive's son?' she hazarded.

'Yes, that's right. The old man's roped me in to help with the drinks tonight. Can I get you one?'

'Thanks, but someone's already gone.'

'Whose daughter are you?' Jon asked. 'I know some of the older generation are bringing their offspring, but I can't remember any called Morgan. Have you been here before?'

'No. No, I haven't. And I'm not . . .'

Andrew emerged from the kitchen, looked round for her and raised a glass in acknowledgement when she waved. He started towards her, but then someone he knew greeted him and he stopped to talk.

'Oh, is that your father?' Jon frowned. 'But isn't that Andrew Naughton? I didn't realise he had a family. Surely he . . .' He stopped suddenly as realisation dawned.

Carly glanced down. 'Definitely a fifteen, I'd say.'

He looked puzzled. 'What is?'

'The size of your foot you just put in it,' she remarked drily.

He gave a boyish, slightly discomfited grin, but then he changed from boy to man in two swift seconds as the grin changed to a knowing smile as his eyes ran over her. 'So you're his girl-friend?'

'His fiancée,' Carly corrected coldly. 'Excuse me, will you?' She turned to go and join Andrew.

'Hey, don't run away.' Jon caught her arm. 'If you get bored any time you only have to say the word,' he said, his voice heavy with suggestion. 'I'll be around.'

'Yes,' Carly agreed sweetly, 'I'll try to remember that—but somehow I don't think I'll be able to wait long enough for you to grow up.'

He didn't like that. His hand tightened on her arm. 'You don't mean to tell me that an old guy like that can keep you satisfied, do you?'

Carly would have liked to hit him, but he was her hosts' son and she couldn't make a scene. Instead she gave him a mocking smile and said dreamily, 'Are you crazy? He's dynamite. Why do you think girls go for older men instead of boys like you?' Then she resolutely shook off his hand and went across to join Andrew. He smiled down at her, gave her a drink and put a possessive arm round her waist. Carly realised that what she'd said to Jon Moresby would probably spread all round the party by the end of the evening and send Andrew's reputation sky-high. He might also hear it himself and she didn't know whether he'd be amused or annoyed. Certainly no one in that room would believe the truth about them.

Carly sighed inwardly. It was by no means the first time that she had come across that attitude from men, they thought that Andrew was marrying her just for sex, and if she was willing to sell herself to him then she must also be willing to come across for other men, although why the one must automatically lead to the other, she couldn't imagine. Some of the men who had made a pass at her had even been supposed friends of Andrew's, but she had never told him and didn't think he had any idea that it happened.

He was talking golf with another member of the
Club, discussing matches and handicaps. He wanted
her to join the ladies' section and she had said she
would after they were married and the business was
established, but now that he was going to be the
Captain for a year she supposed she would have to
join more or less straightaway.

Their fellow guest said something on the same lines.
'Can't have a Captain without a Captain's lady, can we,
m'dear,' he laughed. Then a thought struck him. 'I say,
you are twenty-one, aren't you? We don't admit anyone
under twenty-one for membership. Although perhaps in
this case . . .'

'It's all right, I'm old enough,' Carly told him wryly.

'Good, good. My daughter will be twenty-one in a
few weeks and then she'll be joining, too. You'll be
company for one another.' He didn't seem to find
anything at all incongruous in what he'd said.

They were playing disco music in the garden. Carly
pulled at the back of Andrew's jacket and he got the
message. He took her outside and they began to dance.
If he noticed that his fellow golfer had treated her like a
child, he didn't say anything, probably thinking it best
to ignore it. Perhaps because he still sometimes did it
himself, although not very often.

It was mostly the younger generation that were
dancing, the older people preferred to stand around
talking with drinks in their hands; they wouldn't start
dancing until after the buffet supper, when they had
had wine and a lot more drinks. Carly had noticed that
the older people got, the larger ratio of drinks it seemed
to take to get them going. After a couple of dances,
Andrew took her back inside and they joined the
talkers. Usually Carly didn't mind, but tonight the
sound of the music drifting in through the windows set

her foot tapping and several times she glanced wistfully towards the garden. She wondered what Kyle would be like to dance with, somehow she had the idea that he would be good, willing to let his hair down and dance all night if he was in the mood.

Suddenly she was bored by the party. Leaving Andrew's side, she wandered into the dining-room where the food was laid out. Most of the guests had eaten, but there was still plenty left: the salmon mousse in the shape of a fish with half an olive for its eye, chicken vol-au-vents, four different quiches, dishes full of salad stuff, and trifles, gateaux, and a plate piled high with profiteroles for pudding. Far too much. The Moresbys would be living off the remains for a week. Carly picked up a plate and helped herself to a piece of rich chocolate gateau, pouring a liberal helping of cream over it and to hell with worrying about her figure. A middle-aged woman, who Carly vaguely remembered being introduced as Clive Moresby's older sister, bustled into the room with a tray to collect dirty plates. She frowned as she saw Carly turn to go back into the sitting-room. 'All you young people are eating out in the garden,' she said crossly. 'We don't want food trodden into the carpet.' For all the world as if Carly was about ten years old.

'I'm not a young person,' Carly retorted, stung into losing her temper. 'Can't you tell? I'm old. I'm as old as you are!' Then she slammed the plate down on the table and marched back into the sitting-room.

'Well, really!' The woman gazed after her in shocked astonishment.

Andrew was equally taken aback when she strode up to him and broke into his conversation without apology, saying, 'Andrew, I have a headache and I want to go home. *Now.*'

'What? Er—why, of course. We'll just say goodbye to Clive and Anne.'

'If you'll give me the keys, I'll wait in the car. You can say goodbye for me.'

He looked at her taut face and immediately gave her the keys, coming out to join her in less than five minutes. For a few miles he drove in silence, but then he pulled into a quiet side road and stopped, switching off the lights so that only the moonlight lit the car. The midsummer moon. Carly looked up at it and remembered.

'Do you want to tell me about it?' Andrew asked quietly.

'I told you; I have a headache.'

'No, you haven't.' He reached over and took her hand. 'I know something happened to upset you. Won't you tell me what it is?'

She was silent for a moment, then she burst out, 'I don't know which generation I'm supposed to be in any more! I have to behave like you, but I'm treated like a child!'

'*Have* to behave like me?'

'Well—all right, *try* to behave like you, then. I do my best to be on a level with your friends, but they treat me as if I was one of their children's contemporaries.'

'It's bound to happen, I suppose,' Andrew said reasonably. 'But I'm sure it will be all right when we're married.'

'Why?' she returned petulantly. 'Will people look at my wedding ring and automatically treat me as if I was twenty years older?' Then, horrified, she realised what she'd said and put her hands up to her face. 'Oh God, Andrew, I'm sorry.'

He gave a rather bitter laugh. 'Somebody really did

upset you, didn't they? Who was it, and what did they say?'

'It wasn't just one person. It was a combination of things.' She shrugged. 'I don't know, maybe it's just that I'm over-sensitive tonight. There were so many strangers there.'

'Yes, of course. Or maybe it's pre-wedding nerves. I know I'm getting them very badly.'

Carly recognised the teasing note in his voice and smiled faintly. 'Now that I don't believe; you're never nervous.'

'Of course I am. I just hide it behind a bland exterior, that's all. There are some people who frighten me to death—Mrs Bruton who's on the board of Governors at the grammar school with me, for one. I always feel like a ten-year-old schoolboy again whenever she has a go at me.' Carly laughed, completely unable to imagine it, and he took her hand again. 'That's better. I hate to see you upset. Don't think that I don't understand, Carly. I know it's tough for you—especially now. People make unkind remarks, either because they don't think or because they don't understand.'

'They think I'm cheap,' she said bitterly. 'They think I'm selling myself to you.'

'Only those who're stupid and jealous,' Andrew answered forcefully. 'Not those who know us. Not our friends. And the opinions of the others don't matter. You must try and remember that, Carly. I've told you so before.'

'Yes, I know.' But she sighed.

'It will be all right once we're married,' he reassured her. 'You'll see. Nobody will treat you like a child then.'

'You keep saying that. As if some miracle is going to take place when we walk back up the aisle and everyone

is going to look at us differently, see us in a new light.'
She said it calmly enough, but there was disbelief in her
tone.

Andrew laughed. 'They will, believe me.' He started
up the car. 'Forget about it; those people tonight were
of no importance. We won't go to the Moresbys' again,
won't even see them, if you'd rather not.'

'Oh, it wasn't their fault. Clive and Anne are okay.'
Carly sat back in her seat, looking out of the window as
Andrew covered the short distance into town. The night
was warm again and, as it wasn't very late, there were
still plenty of people about taking advantage of the fine
weather. They came to a road junction where the Green
Dragon, Grantston's one and only Chinese restaurant,
stood on the corner. Andrew stopped and waited to
turn to the right just as a small crowd of people
emerged from the brightly lit doorway of the restaurant.
Carly caught an aroma of spicy, savoury cooking which
made her feel hungry even though she wasn't. The
crowd of people broke up into couples and began to
walk along the road. Carly suddenly grew very tense as
she saw that one of the men was very tall and fair. She
willed him to turn towards her and he did so, almost at
her bidding. It was Kyle, as she'd suspected. He was
wearing his usual jeans and open-necked shirt. And he
had his arm round the waist of a girl who was clinging
to his arm and laughing up at him. He glanced across at
the car and his eyes met hers, but he made no sign of
recognition as they drove away.

'We've arrived.'

Andrew's voice cut through her thoughts. 'What?'
Carly glanced round and saw that they had stopped at
the mews. She got out of the car and they walked down
to her flat. 'Are you coming in for a nightcap?'

Andrew hesitated. 'Are you sure you want me to?'

'Of course.' Unlocking the door, she led the way upstairs but didn't attempt to get him a drink, instead turning to face him. 'Andrew?'

'Yes?'

'I——' She hesitated, then said on a high, urgent note, 'I want you to kiss me. Please kiss me.'

'My dear—of course. But why do . . .'

'Just kiss me, Andrew.' Carly put her arms around his neck as soon as he came close enough and returned his kiss with an ardour and urgency that took him by surprise.

'Carly.' He murmured her name against her mouth. Always he was quickly aroused to passion, and his arms tightened round her. Then his hand was at her clothes, hastily pulling aside the material of her dress until he found her breasts. His breath quickened and grew ragged as he squeezed and fondled, his other hand slipping down to her thighs to press her against him, letting her know that he wanted her. 'Let's go and lie on your bed for a few minutes,' he suggested thickly, freeing her mouth.

'No!' Carly suddenly pulled away from him and went to stand at the window, her hands gripping the sill, her back to him.

'Carly, what is it?'

'Nothing. I . . .' Her voice broke, she shouldn't have gone to the window, it was the one that looked out over the water meadows, silvered by the moonlight, down to the willows that edged the river. Hastily she turned her back on the scene. 'Andrew, do we have to go through with that big wedding? I can't bear the idea of all those people, staring at us.' Going to him, she gripped the lapels of his jacket and gazed earnestly into his face. 'Can't we just go to the Registrar's Office? Just the two of us, tomorrow. Oh, *please*, Andrew!'

He stared at her in frowning astonishment, lifting his

hands to her shoulders. Unable to take the transition from physical need so quickly, he tried to kiss her again, to urge her towards the bedroom.

But Carly angrily broke away. 'You're not listening to me!'

'All right. Okay.' He ran a hand through his dark hair. 'Let's sit down and talk this out. But first I need a drink.' He poured himself a Scotch and went over to a chair by the table and sat down, evidently unable to trust himself if he sat next to her on the settee. 'Come and sit down, and tell me exactly what brought this on.'

Reluctantly Carly obeyed him, but said, 'Do we have to discuss it? Won't you just please do as I ask?'

'Carly, we can't just alter all the arrangements for a whim. You were happy about the wedding up until tonight; what made you change your mind?'

'Men think I'm cheap. They make passes at me,' she said lamely. 'I can't take it any more.'

His face hardened. 'Just tell me who it was and I'll make darn sure they regret it. Who was it?'

'Oh, what does it matter?' She stood up restlessly. 'Please let's get married quickly, Andrew.'

'Tell me who it was,' he insisted.

'Oh, for heaven's sake! Do you want a list of the men who think I'm available because I'm marrying you? Some of the names would surprise you, believe me. But that's not the point. I want to get married in a private ceremony and as soon as possible, not wait until August with half of Grantston staring at us, smirking behind our backs, making insinuations about why we're marrying each other!'

Andrew looked at her in dismay, realising that she was seriously unnerved. Getting to his feet, he came over and took her hands in his. 'Look, why don't you come home with me and spend the night at The Elms?

I'm worried about you and I'll feel much happier if you're under my roof.'

'No.' She shook her head. 'I'd rather stay here.' Carly tried to pull herself together, realising that she was worrying him. 'I'm sorry. I'm not usually so—so female, am I?' She managed a ghost of a smile.

He smiled in return and there was relief in his voice as he said, 'I expect you're tired. You've probably been working too hard with the business. You mustn't let it make you ill, you know. It isn't that important.'

Carly lifted her head to look at him. 'Isn't it?'

'Well, it will only be a hobby for you. It's not as if you'll have to depend on the proceeds.'

'No. No, I suppose not.' She drew away from him. 'I'm rather tired, Andrew.'

'Of course.' He patted her shoulder. 'Get a good night's sleep and I'm sure you'll feel better about things in the morning. I'll phone you about eleven. Goodnight, darling.' He drew her to him and kissed her, said, again with that touch of pleased surprise, 'I didn't know how passionate you could be.'

When he had gone, Carly undressed and put her things away in the wardrobe, saw Kyle's jacket hanging there and reached out to touch it. Then she remembered him with the girl outside the Chinese restaurant and angrily pulled the jacket off its hanger and threw it on the floor. Getting into bed, she pulled the covers over herself and glared at the darkness, but suddenly burst into tears for no reason whatsoever.

At eleven the next morning Andrew phoned as he had promised, sounding worried and anxious, but Carly was able to reassure him that she was quite all right, to laugh and to apologise for being so silly, so that he was completely reassured. He sounded very relieved and insisted that she didn't do any work for the rest of the week. He also had a huge bouquet of flowers sent round via the local florists, so big that Carly had to leave half the flowers in water in the sink because she didn't have enough vases to take them all and had to go out and buy some.

It was market day and the streets were busy, the market attracting people from all the surrounding villages as it did every week. Carly decided she wasn't going to spend a lot on vases which she would probably never use again; Andrew's mother always had flower arrangements in every room at The Elms, so she did the same as every other inhabitant in Grantston did when they wanted something good but inexpensive; she went to the market. It was held where it had always been held since the town had been granted the charter in 1546, on either side of the wide High Street, the lines of stalls under gaily-striped awnings running from the town hall at the top of the street down to what had once been the original grammar school but was now the library and museum at the bottom. Many of the farmers and smallholders still brought their produce in to sell, as had their forebears for generations back, and there were stalls selling homemade cheeses, chutneys and jams as well as those piled high with fruit and vegetables. There were always people selling clothes and household goods, and in recent years these had been augmented by younger people taking stalls to sell their craft products: pottery, canework, enamel jewellery, paintings and artificial flowers.

As usual, the pavements in front of the stalls were thronged with shoppers, baskets and bags over their arms, cheerfully jostling one another to see the wares and eagerly stepping forward whenever a stallholder called out a particular bargain: 'Two pounds of lovely

apples for fifty pence. Here y'are, love, get yer false
teeth stuck into them,' one man called out to an elderly
woman, who laughed goodhumouredly. Another
shouted, 'You'll never believe what I'm asking for this
tea-set. Bone china and fit for the Queen—eighteen
pieces. Just look at 'em!' Carly paused to watch as by
some practised miracle he balanced the whole tea set on
one arm: cups, plates and saucers. 'What am I asking?
Not twenty quid. Not fifteen. Not ten. Seven pounds,
fifty; that's all I'm asking for this beautiful bone china
set. At that price I'm giving it away.' Carly wasn't
surprised when several housewives eagerly opened their
purses to buy; it looked a good bargain. She smiled,
loving the life and bustle of the market, and moved on
down the sunlit street looking for a stall selling cheap
china or pottery vases.

'Ice cream. Home-made ice cream!' a strong male
voice called out, and Carly looked across in surprise,
not having heard that cry in the market before. A little
further down was one of the old-fashioned stop-me-
and-buy-one handcarts, gaily painted and with a red
and white wooden awning. A girl in a sun-top and red-
ribboned boater hat was dishing out the ice cream and
beside her was a man, taller than the awning and
obscured from Carly's view by it. But she had seen the
girl before, coming out of the Chinese restaurant last
night and guessed who the man must be. Her legs
moving of their own volition, Carly walked forward
until she was able to see Kyle clearly. He, too, was
wearing a straw boater and looked to be enjoying
himself immensely as he took the money and dished out
change to the small queue of people at the cart.

Carly stared at him, open-mouthed with astonishment, until he looked up and saw her, then she quickly
turned and began to walk back the way she had come,

pushing past people in her haste to get away. But Kyle muttered something to the girl beside him and came after her. He caught her up just past the hardware shop where there were buckets, brooms and tins of cheap paint piled up outside and where she had been forced to let a woman pushing a pram go by.

'Carly.' He put his hand on her arm.

'Don't touch me!' She jerked her arm away and faced him angrily. 'What do you want?'

'To say hello.' His blue eyes looked her over with disconcerting intentness.

She gazed back at him furiously, wanting to pick a fight. 'You look ridiculous in that hat,' she burst out.

He grinned. 'I know, but it's a part of the uniform.'

'Don't you care about making a fool of yourself in front of the whole of Grantston?' she demanded petulantly.

The grin faded. 'Don't be such a prig. What's wrong with working on a market stall?' She didn't answer, just glared at him, and Kyle said rather grimly, 'Let's go and have a coffee.' This time there was no shaking off his hand as he took a firm grip of her arm and steered her towards the nearest café. They sat in a booth and he squashed in beside her instead of sitting opposite, tossing his hat on to a spare seat. They didn't speak until they had been served with coffee and then he said, quite conversationally, 'Have you broken off your engagement yet?'

Carly didn't even bother to answer that one. 'Your jacket's still at my place,' she said abruptly. 'I'll get someone to bring it to you.'

'Why don't you bring it yourself?'

He moved to stir his coffee and she could feel his shoulder against hers. She bit her lip. 'I told you, I don't want to see you again.'

'You don't have any feelings for me, then?'

'No. None.' Said with as definite a note as she could manage.

'Then you have nothing to be afraid of if you come down to the boat, have you?' Before she could form a protest, he went on, 'I've invited a few friends down to the *Lydia* tomorrow night for a get-together. Why don't you come along then? That's if you're afraid to be alone with me,' he added mockingly.

Carly ignored that last remark. 'What do you mean—a get-together?' she asked suspiciously.

He shrugged. 'Just a few people to have a drink, make some music.'

Carly knew that she was going to refuse and meant to say so straightaway, but somehow she said instead, 'That—that girl you were helping, will she be there?'

'Alison? Yes, I expect so.'

'Then why ask me as well?' she demanded sharply. 'To prove how good you are with women? To show off?'

Kyle turned towards her and put a long finger under her chin. 'Do I detect a note of jealousy there?'

'Certainly not!' She slapped his hand away. 'You seem to make friends very easily, that's all.'

'It isn't difficult when you meet people half-way. I met Alison at the Crown and Anchor, she works part time there as a barmaid. She's trying to set up this home-made ice cream business in the local market, but she's having trouble with the commercial ice cream van driver. He threatened to smash up her cart if she didn't clear out, so I volunteered to come along as a kind of bodyguard.'

Carly felt the muscles in his arm against hers and envied the other girl his protection. 'You'd better get back to her, then,' she said snappily.

'There plenty of time. He can't very well do anything with crowds of people around.' Kyle finished his coffee and turned to face her again. 'When are you going to admit that you're not in love with Andrew?'

'When are you going to shave off your beard and get a job?' she countered, her face tightening.

'If I do that will you give him up?'

She looked down at the table. 'No. You don't understand.'

'Has he some hold over you, Carly?'

'No, of course not. I'm going to marry him and I'm going to make him happy,' she said firmly. 'Can't you get that into your head?'

'What about your happiness? Or doesn't that come into it?'

'Oh, for heaven's sake—I've had enough of this! I'm getting out of here.' Picking up her bag, she turned to slide out of the booth, but Kyle's solid body blocked her way. 'Will you please get out of my way?' she demanded through gritted teeth.

But he remained immovable. 'Will you come tomorrow night?' he asked again, his eyes on her face.

'I've told you—no.'

'What are you afraid of, Carly? Of me—or of losing Andrew?'

'Neither. I could never lose Andrew, and as for you—you mean nothing to me.' But her voice faltered as her eyes met his and held. 'Nothing,' she repeated, lost in his gaze, her voice no more than a whisper, a breath.

A voice broke in on them. 'Why, Carly, we don't often see you in here.'

She turned bemused eyes to see that a girl who had been in her form at the local grammar school had just come into the café. 'I thought you'd be busy preparing for the wedding. Next month, isn't it?' The girl's words were addressed to Carly, but her eyes were on Kyle, taking everything in, not missing a detail, from the lost, glazed look on Carly's face to Kyle's annoyance at her interruption.

'No, in August,' Carly answered mechanically. She got to her feet. 'Here, you can have this table; we're just going.'

'Oh, I don't want to push you out. Why don't you stay and have another coffee with me? It's ages since we've seen each other. And your friend, of course.'

'Sorry, but I have to go. Some other time, perhaps.' Carly nudged Kyle towards the door.

'Oh, I see,' the girl pretended to be offended. 'Too good for an old school friend like me now, are you?' she said in a raised voice.

Carly flushed with embarrassment, unable to answer such direct rudeness, but Kyle merely picked up his boater, put it on his head at a rakish angle and looked down at the other girl. 'It's quite obvious that she always was,' he told her laconically, leaving the girl gaping after him as he followed Carly outside.

When they had gone a few yards, Carly said huffily, 'I can fight my own battles, you know. I don't need you to do it for me.'

'Of course,' he agreed smoothly.

As she looked into his face, her mouth broke into a reluctant grin and then she burst out laughing. 'The look on her face—especially when you put that ridiculous hat on!'

Kyle grinned back at her, then completely silenced her by saying, 'You know, you look beautiful when you laugh. You should do it more often.'

She stared at him, unable even to defend herself. 'I must go.'

He nodded. 'I thought you'd say that. You always

have to leave whenever I say something that makes you start to think about yourself.'

'That isn't true. I have a lot to do today.'

'Oh, sure.' He pushed his silly hat forward so that it almost hid his eyes. 'See you tomorrow night.' Then he turned and walked away from her, pushing through the crowd back to the ice cream cart.

Carly watched him go, thinking even as she stood there that it should have been the other way round, that she should have walked away from him. But something held her until he was hidden from sight by the stalls, then she turned and made her way home, lost in her own thoughts, completely forgetting the vases she had gone out to buy. She remembered when she reached the flat and saw the flowers in the sink, of course, but there was no way she was going to go out into the town again, so she picked up the flowers and took them across the mews to an old lady who lived alone in a ground floor flat. But even this act of charity was a mistake, because the old lady insisted she stay for a cup of tea and tell her all about the plans for her wedding, which Carly wasn't in the mood for right then.

It was an hour before she escaped and went home to finish all the housework that she should have done earlier, but her mind wasn't on it, she kept thinking about Kyle's invitation to the *Lydia* tomorrow night. It was a Saturday and normally Andrew took her out, so she couldn't have gone even if she'd wanted to. Not that she wanted to, of course. Just sitting around drinking and talking with a crowd of strangers, and watching Kyle with that girl, wasn't her idea of fun. She put some shoes away in the wardrobe and saw his jacket lying where she had thrown it. Slowly she reached out and picked it up. He must wear it when he was working on the boat, there was an oil stain on the

sleeve, and when she held it near her face she could
smell traces of oil and paint, all the boating smells
mixed up together. Carly put the jacket back on the
hanger, smoothing it carefully. She still had to get it
back to him somehow; maybe she could pay one of the
young schoolboys who sometimes played in the mews
to take it for her. She certainly wasn't going to take it
herself, and she was equally sure that Kyle wouldn't
come and get it. The thing was getting to be a darn
nuisance, and she wished wholeheartedly that she had
remembered to give it back to him at the time. She'd
definitely see to it tomorrow when the children were on
holiday from school.

At seven that evening Carly drove over to The Elms
for dinner with Andrew and his mother. It was a very
pleasant meal and nothing was said about her outburst
the other night. Andrew might not even have told his
mother about it, but Carly doubted that; the two of
them had a good relationship and usually told each
other most things. And she was left in no doubt at all
when, after dinner, Mrs Naughton determinedly
brought out the pile of blank invitation cards and
insisted they each take a pile and get down to writing
them out. 'There are bound to be lots of people who
aren't able to come because they'll be away on holiday,
so the sooner we have the numbers for the caterers the
better,' she observed.

'All right, I suppose we'll have to get down to it.
Here, you write the invitations and I'll do the
envelopes,' Andrew told Carly, pulling up a chair for
her to sit next to him at a big antique desk, while his
mother made do with a smaller one, in the bay window.

Carly picked up one of the beautifully printed
invitation cards and read it, although she'd seen them
before, of course. Because she had no relations of her

own, they had been sent out in Mrs Naughton's name.
'The wedding of Miss Carly Elaine Morgan to Mr
Andrew Charles Naughton at All Saints Church,
Grantston.' It all sounded very formal and very final.
'Followed by a reception at The Elms.' There were to
be three huge marquees put up on Mrs Naughton's
beautiful lawns, the caterers had been told what food to
provide, and Andrew's wine cellar was already filled by
dozens of cases of champagne that he had got at a good
price through a friend, as he had proudly told her.

Without a word Carly took the pen that Andrew held
out to her and began to fill in the cards: Mr and Mrs G. A.
Graham; Mr and Mrs T. Dixon; the list seemed to be
comprised mainly of married couples, a few of them
adding 'and family' if they were relations of Andrew's.
Only the small group of her own friends seemed to be
mostly for individual people. They all three wrote solidly
for over two hours, but even then they hadn't finished the
invitations. At last Carly dropped the pen on the desk.
'I've had enough,' she declared. 'I'm getting writer's
cramp. Can't we finish them some other time?'

'I quite agree,' Mrs Naughton said from the window.
'But there aren't that many left; I'll try and finish them
over the weekend.'

They talked for a little longer, then Mrs Naughton
tactfully said goodnight and left them alone.

'You're happy with everything again now?' Andrew
asked her.

'Yes, of course. It was just nerves. Thank you for the
flowers, they were beautiful.'

'I'm glad you liked them.' He put his arm round her
waist as he walked her out to the car. There was a breeze
tonight that set the leaves in the elm trees rustling, it
sounded like the river rippling along its banks. Andrew
glanced up at the clear, starlit sky. 'I don't know how long

this hot weather is going to last. It will probably take a few thunderstorms to break it up.'

They reached her car, parked just outside the pool of light thrown by the lamp in the porch, and Andrew drew her to him, kissing her fiercely. 'Last night,' he muttered, 'you were so passionate—you made me want you until it was almost unbearable. Carly darling, you're so lovely.' His hands fondled her, trying to rouse her as he kissed her again, his lips probing.

She pulled away a little. 'Andrew, I . . .'

But he said quickly, 'You said you wanted to get married straightaway. Well, even if we keep to the wedding date, it doesn't mean that we have to wait to go to bed together.'

'But you said that we should wait until we're married,' Carly objected nervously.

'Because I thought that would be better for you, that you'd be happier if we did it that way.' The hands on her waist began to tremble. 'But last night I was sure that you wanted to go ahead. I know I most certainly did. And surely it's this waiting that's making you nervous, not the wedding itself.'

'No, that isn't so. I don't know.' Agitatedly she tried to draw away from him, but he wouldn't let her. 'I don't want to talk about it, Andrew—not now. Please!'

He looked at her with a puzzled frown. 'I don't understand. You seem to have changed lately.'

'No, I haven't. Of course I haven't.'

'Do you still love me?'

'You know I do.' Carly reached up and put her arms round his neck, let him kiss her as he wanted, trying to lose herself in his lovemaking as she had always done before, but tonight she was conscious of wanting him to hurry up and let her go so that she could go home. Of only returning his kisses half-heartedly. But he didn't seem to notice anything was wrong.

When he let her go at last, Andrew said huskily, 'Think about what I said, Carly. There's no need for us to wait.'

'All right. But I—I don't know.'

He opened the car door for her. 'I'll call for you at seven tomorrow. We'll eat out at the Country Club.'

'Oh, I'm sorry, I can't make it tomorrow.' The words came out before Carly even knew she was going to say them. 'I've had an invitation from a friend. A kind of farewell party,' she went on hurriedly, stammering a little as she made the excuse.

'That's a shame. The Rotarians are having a special charity night at the Club tomorrow, I thought I'd told you,' he said complainingly. 'Who is this friend? Can't you get out of it?'

'I promised I'd go. And I can't—can't get in touch.'

'Well, I suppose I'll have to go alone, then.'

They said goodnight and Carly drove off, still amazed at what she'd done. And it was just stupid really, because she still didn't intend to accept Kyle's invitation. But anyway, it would be pleasant to have a Saturday night at home for a change, she couldn't remember the last one she had spent alone, certainly not since she had been going steady with Andrew. She would be able to put her feet up and watch television, perhaps even indulge herself a little with a box of chocolates.

Carly kept assuring herself of this all the next day; in the morning when she went to the hairdressers as usual and had her dark, thick hair blow-dried into its elegantly casual style, in the afternoon when she sorted through her wardrobe and decided to press a very pretty red silk-look skirt with matching top—just because it looked as if it needed it, and even in the evening when she put on the two-piece and carefully make up her face, she was still not going to go. She did, in fact, sit down in front of the television and watch a few programmes, but she was too tense to take anything in and they were just moving pictures that skimmed the surface of her mind. At eight-thirty, she took Kyle's jacket from the wardrobe, checked her appearance in the hall mirror and let herself out of the flat.

There weren't many places for young, single people to go in Grantston. The cinema had closed and become a bingo hall and the squash club had a long waiting list for membership. Sometimes there were discos at the civic hall, but since there had been trouble when a gang of motorbike youths came over from Bristol and picked a fight, these had become even rarer. So the young were more or less forced into the pubs on these hot summer nights and Carly could hear the music from the jukeboxes coming through the open windows as she passed them. There were plenty of people about, taking advantage of the unaccustomed fine weather to go for an evening walk. Her footsteps slowed as she neared the old warehouses and several times she was on the point of turning back, because she knew that what she was doing was utterly stupid, but something made her go on until she reached the Crown and Anchor.

Already there was a small crowd of people in the bar, spilling out into the road. Carly had never been to this particular pub before and didn't fancy going in alone. She hesitated outside and a youth lounging in the doorway tried to chat her up. Luckily she saw a sign advertising a beer garden, so she walked round to the back of the building. Here it was much more pleasant. There were tables and benches set out on the terrace overlooking the river and a small garden where couples with children could have a drink. The *Lydia* was moored in its usual place, but there were no lights showing and she couldn't see anyone on board. Carly began to go towards it uncertainly, but then someone called her name and she looked across to see that Kyle was sitting with a group of people at one of the tables on the terrace. He stood up and came over to her.

'I brought your jacket back,' she said hurriedly, her voice brittle. 'That's all. I can't stay.'

'Okay. Thanks.' Kyle took the jacket from her, his eyes on her flushed cheeks. She looked to see if there was any mockery in his face, but there wasn't. 'Won't you at least have a drink before you go, it's a very warm night?'

'Well, just one, then.' She let him lead her back to the table where he introduced her to the other people there, none of whose names she took in, but the girl Alison wasn't among them. Then he sat her in the space next to his and went into the bar to get her a drink. Immediately she felt overdressed and out of place, all the others were wearing shorts and not much else.

The others, about five people, looked at her with deep but slightly guarded curiosity. 'You live round here?' one asked.

'Yes.'

'What do you do?'

'I—I design clothes.'

'Really?' One girl was immediately interested. 'Are you having any luck? I design and make hand-knitted sweaters. I'm having a terrible time in this weather, of course,' she added with a glum laugh.

Kyle came back and sat down next to her and the conversation became general. It seemed that all the people at the table were craft workers of some kind who had rented out space in the nearby warehouses and were trying to make a living out of their talents. Some of them were self-taught, one or two had been to art college as she had. They were all keenly interested when she mentioned that she was starting up her own business, and without realising it, Carly soon found herself talking eagerly, discussing problems, listening, making suggestions. But some instinct made her keep quiet about the help that Andrew was giving her—somehow it seemed an unfair advantage over the others. Kyle joined in occasionally, but he seemed content to mostly listen. Once or twice, Carly turned in his direction and found him watching her, his eyes intent. And at some point his arm went round her and stayed there.

They had more rounds of drinks, and after two or three, Carly reached for her bag. 'Please, let me, it must be my round.'

But Kyle's arm tightened round her waist. 'You're with me,' he said, his blue eyes holding hers, so that for a while she lost the thread of the conversation.

When the pub closed at eleven, they were joined by Alison, who complained of being rushed off her feet all night and longing to sit down, so they all adjourned to the comfortable day cabin of the *Lydia*, where Kyle became the host, bringing out cans of cool beer from the fridge and rolls with thick wedges of ham or cheese that he had made earlier. Carly didn't feel in the least out of place any more, and she had laughed as much as the others when she had tried to board the boat in her high heels and would have tripped if Kyle hadn't caught her. She ate hungrily, drank thirstily, savouring every mouthful as if she had been at the Savoy.

Alison sat next to her and Carly listened sympathetically as the other girl told her all about her ice cream cart and the trouble she was having with the commercials. 'It will be all right when my boy-friend comes home, of course. He's in America at the moment; gone to find out about all those marvellous ice cream parlours they have over there.'

'Oh, you have a boy-friend?'

'Yes.' Alison grinned at her. 'I was only borrowing Kyle. That rotten ice cream van driver nearly died when he saw how big Kyle was!'

Carly laughed, imagining the scene. 'I wish I'd seen it!' She looked across to where Kyle was getting more drinks from his fridge to pass round. He caught her eye and grinned, gave a small wink.

Alison saw the brief exchange and reached out to point at Carly's engagement ring. 'Is that for real? It looks like the rock of Gibraltar!'

'Oh, yes, I think so.' Carly put her hand under the table, feeling guilty at flaunting such affluence when everyone else was struggling so hard to make a living.

'Are you and Kyle engaged, then?'

Carly flushed, groping for words to explain, but Kyle came back and answered for her. 'No, we're not. Carly is engaged to someone else—at the moment. But I'm working on her,' he added, putting an arm round her waist and drawing her closer to him. 'And I think I might even be getting somewhere,' he added softly, for her alone to hear.

Her eyes held by his, Carly didn't attempt to deny it. She merely gave a small smile and settled comfortably against him. One of the men had brought a guitar with him, he started to play and soon they were all singing, swaying to the more melodious tunes or listening in spellbound contentment when he played the slow classical pieces. Carly loved it all; she leant against Kyle's broad shoulder and sang or listened dreamily.

It was as if she was back at college among her contemporaries again, only better, much, much better. Other people came in; the landlady from the pub, a friend of one of the girls, a couple from another boat; Kyle welcomed them all and somehow they squeezed in and found a place to sit, even if it was only on the floor. To make more room Kyle pulled her on to his lap. Carly put an arm round his neck to balance herself, her heart starting to race stupidly when she found his face so close to hers, could feel the warmth and hardness of his thighs pressing against her.

The party went on for hours and she loved every minute of it; they were nearly all young and talented, intelligent people and they had lots to say and tell. They told silly stories in between the songs, and the landlady turned out to have been on the stage in her youth and delighted them all by giving them her 'act' where she pretended to be a ragged doll that kept flopping about.

At last they broke up and the others went home. Carly stayed behind to help Kyle clear up, but she had hardly started before he said firmly, 'Leave that.' He took the glass she was holding from her suddenly shaky hand and put it on the table, then he drew her towards him. 'I'm glad you came back.'

'You said you knew I would.'

'Yes.'

'Why? How could you have known?'

'Because I wanted you to so much.'

'But if I hadn't come—what would you have done?'

He smiled slowly and didn't answer. He put a hand on either side of her head, his eyes fixed on her face, then slowly lowered his head to kiss her, taking her mouth lingeringly, like a man who is drinking the most precious wine the world has ever known.

They kissed for a long time, exploring each other's

mouths, tasting, learning, and all the time the emotion Carly felt grew deeper, more sensual, until she was trembling uncontrollably. When he lifted his head, she slowly opened her eyes and looked into Kyle's face. He was still holding her head a prisoner in his hands and she knew at once from the tautness in his face and the tension in his hands that his feelings went as deep as hers. She knew that he wanted her, at least as much as Andrew had the other night, but Andrew had been rough in his passion, feeling that to show it he had to be tough and hurt her a little, to prove his strength and masculinity. But Kyle, for all his size, hadn't hurt her, and she realised that a man had first to be very strong before he could allow himself to be gentle.

'Oh, Kyle!' She breathed his name on a long sigh.

'Will you stay?'

Three words that could alter her whole life if she said yes, if she gave way to these feelings that threatened to engulf her. Biting her lip, she looked away. 'I can't.'

'Can't? Does that mean that you want to?'

'Whether I want to—or not, doesn't come into it. You know I can't.'

'I don't mean just for tonight. It goes deeper than that.'

'Yes—I know.'

'So stay, Carly. Do what your heart tells you,' he said urgently.

'Don't—please.' She shook her head. 'We can't ever be more than friends. You know I'm going to marry Andrew.'

His calm shaken, Kyle said angrily, 'You mean you're going to throw your future away on a man old enough to be your father! Why? For God's sake just tell me why.'

Very close to tears, Carly answered on a sob, 'Can't you understand? Hasn't it even occurred to you? I'm going to marry him because I love him.' Then she turned and stumbled out of the cabin, leaving him staring after her.

CHAPTER FIVE

IT was almost two weeks before Andrew found out about Kyle. Carly was only surprised that it had taken that long; the Grantston grapevine must slow up during the summer months.

Andrew came over to the flat unexpectedly one evening. It was quite early, only about eight-thirty, and not even beginning to get dark. Carly opened the door to his ring and looked at him in surprise, noting that he was still in his casual golfing clothes. 'Hallo, Andrew. Come in. How did the golf match go?'

She went ahead of him up the stairs and he didn't answer until they were in the sitting-room. 'Quite well. My partner and I won by two holes.'

'Good. You must be pleased. Would you like a drink of something?'

'Er—no, I don't think so.' He seemed ill at ease and didn't sit down, paced restlessly around the room.

Carly had been cutting out paper to make a pattern for her dressmakers to work to and had the work spread out on the floor as well as her worktable. She began to quickly pick the pieces of paper up off the floor as she knew that he didn't like untidiness. 'Sorry the place is in such a mess,' she apologised. 'It won't take me a minute to clear up.'

'It doesn't matter. I hope you don't mind me calling round. Perhaps I should have phoned first?'

There was something in his voice that made her glance at him. His face was tense and the lines that had begun to show running down towards his mouth were etched deeper. Intuitively Carly knew what had happened and braced herself to take it. As steadily as she could, she said, 'Why phone? You know you can always come here whenever you want to.'

'Do I?' The question was loaded.

'Of course. I don't have to tell you, surely?'

Andrew ran a hand through his hair, then smoothed it again, a gesture he only used when he wasn't completely sure of himself. He had made that same gesture a dozen times the night he had decided to propose to her. Not that he need have worried, Carly had realised what was coming and knew that her only answer could be yes. It was the only way she could ever repay him for what he had done for her. He cleared his throat.

'Mother went to a bridge party yesterday afternoon,' he told her. 'She heard something rather—er—surprising. She told me, but we decided that it was just gossip. You know how it is at bridge parties.' Carly didn't, but she could well imagine it. 'We decided to forget it,' Andrew went on. 'But then I overheard something at the clubhouse this evening. Something I wasn't supposed to hear.'

Biting her lip, Carly turned away and pretended to gather up the pieces of paper on her worktable, her hands shaking a little. Poor Andrew! She could imagine someone at the Golf Club who didn't like him or was jealous of him, deliberately making a snide remark about her going with another man so that Andrew would hear. She would have given anything for it not to have happened that way—for it not to have happened at all. But in a place like this it had been inevitable. 'Really? What about?'

'About you.' Andrew came over to the table and caught her hand. 'Look at me, Carly.'

Slowly she put down the papers she was holding and obeyed him, trying to keep her gaze steady and unashamed. After all, she had nothing to feel really guilty about. But she wished with all her heart that Andrew would let the matter drop.

He looked intently into her face. 'Mother and I both heard, from separate sources, that you'd been seen with another man.'

'Seen with? What does that mean?'

'Well, what do you think it means?' Andrew retorted rather harshly, beginning to lose his cool. 'You were seen with a man in the town, some hippie, by all accounts. And someone else saw you in a café with him. At least, it sounds like the same man. Well?' he almost barked at her. 'Aren't you going to explain?' Carly looked at him silently, and he added blusteringly, 'I know it was completely innocent, of course, but I would . . .'

'If you know that,' she interrupted, 'why have you come here? Why are you questioning me?'

He looked taken aback. 'People are talking about you. Making insinuations.'

'Insinuations?' She put a hand over his where he still held her and gazed up at him. 'Andrew, do you trust me?'

'Why, yes, I suppose so.'

'Are you sure? Do you *really* trust me?'

After looking at her silently for a long moment, he sighed and said, 'Yes. Yes, of course I do.'

'Then please, let's drop this, Andrew.'

'Just like that?' he sounded incredulous. 'Without any kind of an explanation?'

'If you trust someone you don't have to demand explanations,' Carly pointed out tartly, moving away. 'I know that you sometimes see other women, but I don't ask you for explanations.'

'That's either business or to do with one of the organisations I belong to. And you know it.'

'No, I don't *know* it—but I'm willing to take it on trust.'

There was heightened colour in his cheeks as he followed her across the room. 'Don't try to change the subject, Carly. I want to know who this man is and—and what he means to you.'

'He doesn't mean anything to me.' Turning her back on him, she poured herself a drink from the tray on the sideboard with an unsteady hand. 'Do you want a drink?'

'No. How long have you known him?'

'Not long. About three weeks.' She screwed the tops back on the bottles, unwilling to face him.

Andrew was silent for a moment, then, 'I said that you seem to have changed lately; is it because you've met this man?'

Taking a long swallow of her drink, Carly sat down in the armchair and tried to speak calmly. 'I haven't changed; it was just nerves, like I told you.'

'It seemed a whole lot more than nerves to me.' She didn't answer and he went on harshly, 'You still haven't told me who he is.'

'Because it doesn't matter!' Slamming her drink down on the coffee table, Carly got up and moved restlessly around the room. 'For heaven's sake, Andrew, can't you drop this? Surely you can see that it isn't doing any good?'

'I want to know,' he demanded stubbornly, angry again. 'Tell me who he is. I suppose he's young?'

'All right!' She turned to face him, angry in her turn. 'If you really want to know every detail. His name is Kyle Anderson, and no, he isn't young; he's quite old, nearly thirty.'

Andrew flinched at that and she could have bitten out her tongue, but it was too late to take it back. 'I see,' he said harshly. 'So what the hell does that make me?'

Carly was close to tears, but she tried hard to control herself. 'Please, Andrew. He was just someone I met quite by accident and ran into a few times. Okay, he was nice and I liked him. But I *love* you and I'm going to *marry* you.'

But her words had little effect. The pinched look was still round his mouth as he demanded in a grim, unsteady voice, 'Have you been to bed with him? Have you?'

Her face chalk white, Carly crossed to the door and pulled it open. 'Goodbye, Andrew.'

'What—what do you mean?'

Her eyes filled with angry tears, but she managed to hold them in check. 'If you can—if you can ask me a question like that, then there's no point in going on. We might as well end it now.'

'No!' He strode quickly across and pushed the door shut with a violent slam, then put his hands on her arms, gripping tightly. 'I'm—I'm sorry. I shouldn't have asked that. It was unforgivable. But can't you understand? Don't you realise how jealous it makes me feel when I hear about you with another man—a younger man?'

'I've told you that I love you and want to marry you; what more can I say?' asked Carly with a helpless shrug.

'Will you promise not to see this man again?' Andrew said eagerly, his fingers digging into her. 'You must.'

She looked at him in some astonishment, the thought occurring to her that that was the kind of thing a strict father would demand, not a boy-friend. 'But why?' she protested. 'You either believe me or you don't.'

'I do believe you—truly. But people are talking

already. If you're seen in his company again—well, you can imagine what people would say.'

'Is that all you're worried about—what other people say?' she asked with a trace of bitterness.

'You know it's not.' He looked intently into her face and she felt instantly ashamed.

'I'm sorry.' Tiredly, she moved away from him and crossed to the table, picked up pieces of pattern paper and put them together at random. 'You really have nothing to worry about, you know. I haven't seen Kyle for over a week and it's unlikely that I'll run into him again. Anyway, he may be gone by now. He doesn't live here, he's just—visiting for a while.'

'So you won't see him again?'

Annoyed by his need for reassurance, Carly said shortly, 'I'm not going to promise, if that's what you mean. If he's still in Grantston then it's possible that I might run into him, and I'm not going to just ignore him to placate all the gossipmongers. He's a friend of mine, and I don't ignore my friends. Next you'll be trying to make me promise not to see any of my college friends again—if they happen to be male, that is.' Which was hardly fair, but Carly didn't like being pushed into a corner.

'I've never objected to you seeing any of your friends. But this is different.'

'Is it? Or are you making it so?'

His brows drew together in puzzlement for a moment, then he glared at her. 'Don't try and push the blame on me, Carly, that won't work. I'm very disappointed by your attitude. I can't make you promise, but if you love me as you say you do, then I think you would have given your word willingly. And I won't demand it of you. I don't think I have the right to do that, even though we're engaged.'

Her throat tightened with emotion and Carly
turned away, the tears that had been threatening all
during their row, spilling over. Her shoulders shook
as she said on a smothered sob, 'You—you'd better
go, Andrew.'

'Are you crying?' Putting his hands on her shoulders,
he turned her round to face him. 'Darling, I'm sorry. I
didn't mean to upset you. I'm so sorry.' He pulled her
to him and held her against his shoulder, his arms
round her. 'But can't you see how I feel? The thought of
losing you ... It would drive me insane!' His hands
shook as he held her and he spoke with intense
emotion. 'I couldn't bear it if I lost you. My life
wouldn't be worth living.'

'Oh, Andrew, don't, please. I'm sorry—I'm so sorry.'
She put a hand up to touch his face and he kissed her
fiercely. Carly returned it as ardently as she knew how,
knowing that that was the only real way she could
reassure him. She felt terribly guilty, knowing that this
was all her fault, and told him over and over again that
she loved him and that there was no one but him that
she cared about. He went on kissing her, but gradually
they became less desperate, more possessive, and she
knew that she had convinced him at last. When he at
length let her go she smiled tremulously up at him and
said, 'Now, will you have a drink?' And he smiled and
assented.

They sat together on the settee, very close, holding
hands, both of them consciously making the effort to
get back to their old footing, but their row was too
close for either to relax. Andrew started to talk about
the wedding, about the acceptances that were already
starting to come in, even some wedding presents, and
Carly tried to respond but felt completely drained both
mentally and physically.

After a while Andrew kissed her again and said, 'You know what we were talking about a couple of weeks ago—about not waiting until the wedding? Have you thought about it?'

'No, not really . . .'

His hand moved to the buttons of her blouse. 'Maybe tonight would be a good time to . . .'

'Oh, no! Not tonight.' Her eyes grew dark with distress. 'That would only be just making up after a fight. Not—not love. Can't you see that?'

'Yes, of course. I shouldn't have suggested it,' Andrew said quickly. 'But I do want you, darling. You don't know how difficult it is for a man to have to wait. To be able to hold you and touch you and yet not to be able to go the whole way.'

Carly sat forward on the settee. 'You were willing to wait before.'

His hands were on her back, stroking her. 'Why don't I come round here on Saturday night, and instead of going out we'll have a meal here? I'll bring a couple of bottles of champagne and . . .'

Carly sprang up and turned angrily to face him. 'Why? Because you think I'll say yes more easily if you get me drunk?'

Andrew's face hardened and he stood up. 'You're obviously not in a reasonable mood,' he said shortly. 'I'll phone you tomorrow. And in the meantime perhaps you'd try to be a little more circumspect with your so-called friends.'

She had begun to feel guilty again, but at that her chin came up and she bit back the apology she had been about to make. Instead of seeing him to the door as she always did, she stayed where she was and said, 'Goodnight, Andrew. I'm sure you won't mind seeing yourself out, will you?'

He hesitated for a moment, then turned on his heel and left.

Carly stayed sitting on the settee for a long time, feeling absolutely wretched. She had never even approached having a row with Andrew before and she had never felt so guilty about anything in her life; if she had been strong-willed enough not to have anything to do with Kyle in the first place none of this would have happened. But mixed up with the guilt there was a subconscious anger and rebellion. After all, she had done nothing really wrong, just returned a couple of kisses, that was all. Maybe she had been stupid to get friendly with Kyle, and it had definitely been stupid to go on that boat ride on Midsummer's Eve, but she had done nothing wrong, not in the way that Andrew meant. Did he really believe that she was the kind of person who would have sex with another man when she was engaged to him?

That thought, too, made her angry, but it also made her wonder what it would be like to go to bed with Kyle. Her cheeks reddened as she remembered Kyle's kisses and she had no doubt whatsoever that he would be a very experienced and skilful lover. She jumped to her feet, angry with herself for being unfaithful to Andrew even in her thoughts; especially as it had never once occurred to her to wonder what Andrew would be like in bed. She had often thought about what their life would be like together after they were married, of course, and had liked the prospect of the security and companionship it would give her, but somehow her mind had shied away from the sexual side of it, perhaps because she couldn't begin to envisage what it would be like past the caressing and fondling that was as far as they had ever gone.

Which brought her back to Andrew's wish to have sex before their marriage. In the back of her mind she had hoped that Andrew would forget it, but he had been more pressing tonight and she knew that she would have to make a decision. Should she let him on Saturday or not? Carly paced the room, her arms folded across her chest, and laughed aloud rather hysterically. God, what a decision to have to make! Do I cold-bloodedly offer myself to my fiancé, or do I coyly make him wait till the wedding night? *Oh, hell!* Angrily she flounced into her bedroom, found a jacket and pulled it on, then hurried out of the flat, feeling shut in by it. If she didn't have some fresh air she'd go mad.

Deliberately she turned her footsteps away from the river, heading for the shopping area of the town where she would be able to look in the brightly lit windows. There were plenty of people around, taking an evening stroll as she was. It was only ten o'clock and the sky was still lit by the last rays of a brilliant sunset, promising another fine day tomorrow. Carly strolled aimlessly, window-shopping a little, but her mind a crazy mixture of wishes, regrets, and indecision. She supposed that when Andrew came on Saturday she would say yes, for the simple reason that she had never said no to him before. Always she had let him guide her because he had always known what was best for her. And if he wanted it what right had she to say no?

'Carly! Hi there.'

Turning from an absentminded perusal of a window, Carly saw someone waving to her from across the street. It was Alison, and she had a man with her, a stranger. She waved back and would have walked on, but Alison pulled her companion across to speak to her.

'This is my boy-friend, Gary. He just got back from America a couple of days ago,' she informed Carly with a touch of pride.

He was a nice-looking young man with glasses and a

high forehead. When Carly asked him how he had got on in America he launched into a long account of the ice cream business, but after a few minutes Alison interrupted him. 'You can tell her all about that later. We're going to the Chinese,' she told Carly, putting a hand on her arm. 'Come and eat with us.'

'Oh, no, I'd only be in the way. You must have loads to talk about.'

'Don't be silly; friends are never in the way.' She laughed. 'And besides, I've already heard it all, but Gary would love to have a new audience. Wouldn't you?' she added, turning to her boy-friend.

He grinned goodnaturedly. 'Of course.'

'Good. Then that's settled.' Alison linked her arm in Carly's and pulled her firmly along with them.

She supposed she should have resisted, but Carly was glad of the company; it wasn't as if she went out to work and had people to chat to there; the women who worked for her were older than herself, married and with children, and she had little in common with them apart from the clothes, so she quite often felt lonely. And never more so than tonight, after her row with Andrew, so she went along willingly enough.

They could smell the Green Dragon even before they reached it. The door was wide open on this warm night and the Chinese lanterns in the windows cast weird, coloured shadows on the pavement. It was already quite full, the atmosphere warm and companionable as people laughed and talked above the clatter of the cutlery and the chink of glasses. Carly had never been inside the Green Dragon before; it wasn't the kind of place that Andrew ever went to, and she looked round at the Westernised idea of Chinese decoration with interest.

'Oh look, there's Jane and Tony,' Alison exclaimed,

lifting a hand to wave at a couple Carly recognised from the crowd who had been at the Crown and Anchor. 'Let's go and sit with them.'

The restaurant seemed to be another of the meeting places for all the craftworkers at the warehouses, and the waiters good-naturedly pushed two tables together so that they could sit with their friends. They exchanged greetings and were soon listening to Gary's description of his visit to the States and the ideas that he had got for their ice cream business. Alison excused herself after a few minutes, saying that she'd heard it all before, and went away to powder her nose. When she came back, they spent quite some time arguing about what they should choose to eat, finally ending up with a selection that Carly very much doubted they could possibly get through, but the spicy smells made them all feel hungrier than they really were.

'There's really fantastic scope in this country for the American style ice cream parlours,' Gary was telling them enthusiastically. 'But it's like everything else; you've got to have capital before you can get anywhere.'

'If you can get enough to start one shop and make a success of that, the second will be easy,' Tony joined in.

'Hey, hold your horses—all we've got at the moment is one cart!' Alison pointed out, forever practical.

Carly smiled at their argument, and looked towards the doorway as someone came in. Her breath caught in her throat as she saw that it was Kyle. Every time she saw him she was newly taken aback by his size. He filled the door frame, in width as well as height, and all heads turned towards him as he looked round the restaurant, his eyes searching until he came to their table and settled on her face. Carly felt her heart jump as if she'd had an electric shock, and then beat so

loudly it deafened every other sound. His blue eyes
locked on hers and held them as Kyle walked through
the restaurant and slid into the seat beside her. Carly
tried to drag her eyes away, but she couldn't. She was
aware of nothing but his closeness, and the old cliché of
being alone in a crowded room came true for her for
the first time in her life.

Kyle didn't speak at first, his eyes were intent on her
face, going over each feature, and then he leant forward
and kissed her on the mouth.

The sense of her surroundings came dimly back to
her as Carly slowly opened her eyes; she became aware
of the noise of the restaurant and the silence at their
own table as the other four gazed at them in open-
mouthed astonishment, making Carly's cheeks suffuse
with colour.

Alison immediately came to her rescue by greeting
Kyle and she was able to recover some of her
composure, but all the time she was terribly aware of
him and had to fight an almost overwhelming urge to
constantly touch him, to make sure he was really there.
The meal came and they ate hot curry and spicy spare
ribs, drank a lot of wine and talked until they were dry
again. Sometimes they did touch, by accident, when
Kyle shifted on his chair and his knee brushed against
hers or when he passed a dish and his fingers covered
hers for a brief second. But even that was enough to set
her pulses racing. And when they had finished eating
and were on the first of several cups of coffee, Kyle
deliberately reached under the table and found her
hand, held it firmly in his, their fingers entwined.

She knew she should have pulled away, but knowing
it and being able to do it were quite incompatible. She
knew she ought to have left the restaurant the moment
that Kyle walked in, but she hadn't, her heart had been

too full of emotion to even move: joy at seeing him and an overwhelming relief that he was still in Grantston and hadn't sailed on to another river, another town. Which was completely crazy, of course; she should have hoped that he had gone, that his disturbing presence was out of her life for good and she could settle quietly back as she was before, glad that the ripple he had made could gradually fade away into nothing and be forgotten. But then she had seen him—so tall, so fair, so *magnetic*.

Her hand tightened involuntarily and Kyle turned to look at her. What he saw in her face lit an answering flame in his eyes. 'Let's go,' he said softly.

In a trancelike state, she nodded and they said goodbye to the others, who watched them go in a speculative silence. Kyle paid the bill and then they were out on the street and walking side by side, making Carly remember when she had looked out of the window of Andrew's car and seen Kyle and Alison and got entirely the wrong impression. Her eyes went to the cars that passed them in the street; any one of them could carry someone who knew her and Andrew. Would they see her and Kyle and again get the wrong impression? But then Kyle put his arm round her waist and she forgot to care about being seen with him, about Andrew and everything else.

They strolled into the park, past the grassy mound that was all that was left of an ancient castle and through an arcade hung with wisteria, pale and lovely in the moonlight, the scent of the flowers increased in the stillness of the night. Of common accord, they turned to follow a small stream that had once been the castle moat and was now merely a tributary of the main river, and stopped where the spreading branches of a huge oak cut off the light of the moon and left a cave of darkness.

Kyle turned her round to face him, his hands low on her hips. 'I missed you,' he said huskily.

She didn't try to pretend. 'I know. I missed you too.'

His hand came up to gently touch her face, trace the outline of her cheek and her chin, and Carly sighed languorously. Her lips parted sensuously as he touched her mouth with his fingertip, following the bow of her upper lip, exploring the fullness of the lower that gave a hint of the passion that no man had yet fully awakened. She caught hold of his hand when he would have moved it and held it prisoner, gently kissing each finger, feeling their hard, steel-like strength. There were small callouses on his palm through working on the boat, and she kissed them gently, then ran her tongue between each finger joint and felt his hand quiver in response. His hand took hers, covered it, then moved round to her palm, feeling its softness. It was her right hand and there were no rings to mar his exploration as his big hand entwined with her small one and he lifted it to his mouth to kiss, then gently bit at the soft pouch at the Mount of Venus between her thumb and first finger.

Carly gave a little gasp and his hand tightened. 'Carly . . .'

But she quickly freed her hands and shoved them into the pockets of her jacket as she took a few steps away from him. 'I had a terrible row with Andrew tonight,' she blurted out. 'I've—I've never rowed with him before.'

Kyle slowly closed his empty hand. 'What about?' he asked, a wry note in his voice.

'About you.'

He looked at her quickly. 'Me? How can he possibly know about me? Unless you told him,' he added, his eyebrows rising.

Carly laughed rather sardonically. 'I didn't have to

tell him. You don't know Grantston; nothing ever happens here without the whole town knowing about it. We were seen together. And he heard about it from two different sources. One was his mother,' she added tiredly.

'I see. What did he say?'

'He wasn't very pleased. He wanted to know all about you.'

'And you told him?' Kyle's voice sharpened.

'A little. Not everything.'

He was silent a moment, working out the implications. 'And you rowed?'

'Yes. He—he tried to make me promise never to see you again.'

Kyle came up to her and drew her into the moonlight so that he could see her face. 'But you refused?' he said softly.

'Yes.' His fingers tightened on her arms and he started to pull her towards him, but Carly put her hands against his chest and said quickly, 'I refused because I didn't think he had the right to ask that of me, not for—for any other reason.'

Instantly his fingers relaxed and his mouth twisted a little. 'Go on. How did it end?'

Carly hesitated, wondering whether to tell him. It wasn't the kind of thing you discussed with a man, but she had no one else to confide in.

Noticing her hesitation, Kyle said forcefully, 'Tell me, Carly. Is it all over between you two?'

'Oh no! He—he gave me a kind of ultimatum. He wants to—to make love to me before the wedding,' she stammered. 'He wants to come round to the flat on Saturday. And I don't know what to do,' she finished on a burst of candour.

Kyle was staring at her incredulously. 'Do you mean to tell me he's never made love to you?'

'No.' She shifted uncomfortably. 'We were going to wait until the wedding. But now . . .'

'But now he doesn't want to wait,' Kyle finished for her. 'Because of me?' he demanded, his voice grim.

Carly was about to deny it, but then remembered that the passion she had shown Andrew and made him change his mind had been purely a release of the pent-up emotions Kyle had awoken in her. 'Yes, I suppose so. Indirectly.'

'And what if you refuse?'

She shrugged helplessly. 'How can I refuse? The wedding is only weeks away. No one waits until they're married nowadays, if they're committed to the relationship.'

'Do you want to?'

She turned her face away from the revealing rays of the moon. 'I don't know,' she admitted miserably.

'My God, Carly! How the hell can you possibly marry a man you don't even want to go to bed with?'

'I didn't say that,' she denied. 'It's just—just . . .' Her voice trailed away helplessly.

Angrily he caught hold of her wrist and swung her round to face him, saying harshly, 'He's blackmailing you.'

'What?' She gazed at him in amazement. 'Of course he isn't blackmailing me!'

'Not the kind you mean. I mean moral blackmail. Where one person uses the emotions or guilt of the other to get what they want. That's what your precious boy-friend is doing with you; making you feel guilty so that you'll let him make love to you, and then you'll have no choice but to marry him.'

'That's silly. I'm going to marry him anyway.'

'Are you, Carly? Are you really going to marry a man who doesn't even turn you on?'

'He does turn me on. Of course he does,' she said over-emphatically. 'And besides, sex isn't everything in a marriage. There are other things.'

'But sex happens to be a hell of an important thing,' Kyle pointed out bluntly, adding exasperatedly, 'For heaven's sake, Carly, why don't you admit that you lied to me the other night? He's old enough to be your father. You can't possibly love him.'

Stung, Carly retorted, 'Well, that's just where you're wrong, because I do love Andrew. Very much. And anyway, you're not exactly young yourself.'

'Maybe not,' he agreed tersely, 'but at least I know how to make you feel like a woman!' His eyes darkening, he pulled her into his arms.

'Oh no! Don't, Kyle, please!'

But her words were lost as his mouth took hers, kissing her with a pent-up anger that somewhere along the line changed to passion as his dominant masculinity demanded and got a response. Carly's mouth trembled under his as the world began to spin around her. She was lost, lost in a vortex of time where nothing was real except their closeness, where nothing mattered but the need to return his kiss. Her eyes closed and she felt as if she was falling, her senses reeling under the shock of sheer sexual pleasure. The fire that he had briefly lit grew into a flame of desire that made her tremble with awareness. He held her against him and she didn't resist, she could feel the strength and warmth of his body and knew that he wanted her as she felt the tension growing in him. Her own body betrayed her, her hips moving against his in an agony of frustrated need and she moaned, her mouth opening under his.

'Carly! Oh God, Carly.' His lips left hers to follow the curve of her chin, the hollows of her cheeks, her eyes, her throat, his breath ragged. '*Now* do you realise what it can be like? Do you?' he demanded thickly.

Slowly she opened her eyes, her body still quivering with emotion, and saw the triumph in his face. Putting her hands against his chest, she pushed him violently away from her, catching him off balance so that he fell back a couple of paces. 'Oh yes,' she said bitterly, 'I realise all right. Now for the rest of my life I'll always know that there's something missing from a relationship that would otherwise have been perfectly contented. Until you came along and decided that you just had to try out your masculine virility on me!'

CHAPTER SIX

KYLE stared at her for a minute, completely unprepared for her reaction, then burst out, 'You don't mean you're going ahead with it? Not after this?'

'Of course I'm going ahead with it,' Carly answered stubbornly. 'You don't seriously expect me to change my whole life just because you kissed me, do you?'

'No, not just because I kissed you. But because of what that kiss meant to you.' He stepped towards her again, but Carly moved quickly away.

'It—it didn't mean anything to me.'

'Liar! You're already admitted that it did. Or perhaps it's just that you want another demonstration,' Kyle said tauntingly, reaching for her wrist and pulling her to him.

'No! Don't!' Carly knew that she wouldn't be able to resist him once his mouth touched hers, and so had to fight him with words. 'All right, I admit it. It did mean something, but . . .'

'And I mean something?' His grip tightened on her wrist.

But Carly wasn't willing to concede that much. 'I don't know. Maybe you could, if I wasn't already committed to Andrew. If you'd come along before—before Andrew asked me to marry him, then I might have . . .' She shrugged. 'But it's too late now.'

'No, it's not. You're not married to him yet, only engaged. And engagements can be broken when you realise that you've made a mistake,' he told her forcefully.

'But I haven't *made* a mistake. Meeting you hasn't made me feel any differently about Andrew. He's still the most important person in my life and I care about him very deeply. Nothing can change that.'

Kyle's jaw tightened, but he said, 'Care about him, yes, but you're not in love with him, Carly.'

'It's the same thing, surely?'

He gave her wrist an impatient shake. 'Of course it isn't. Being in love is thinking about the other person all the time, of longing to be with them when you're apart; it's counting the hours until you're together and your heart skipping a beat when you see them. It's an aching need deep in your stomach, an overwhelming longing to touch and be touched by the one you love. And above all,' he went on softly, pulling her closer to him, 'it's what you felt when we kissed just now—that dizzy passion that you never want to end. That need to be a part of each other.'

Carly took a deep, unsteady breath. 'Are you—are you saying that I'm in love with you, then?'

His eyes tried to search her face, but the moon had shifted, leaving her in shadow. Carefully he said, 'Yes, if that's the way you feel about me. You obviously don't feel it about Andrew.'

He waited, his body tense, for her reply, but at length Carly said coldly, 'You seem to know an awful lot about this love thing. I suppose you're always having girls fall for you?' Pulling her hand free, she walked away from him along the path, stopping at the rose-bordered steps leading down to a broad sweep of lawn.

After a moment, Kyle followed her and leant against a wooden post, his hands in the pockets of his jeans, the material stretched tight across his thighs. 'If you hadn't already assured me that I mean nothing to you,' he said drily, 'I'd have noticed more than a little jealousy in that remark.'

'I'm not jealous of you,' Carly returned. 'How could I be? I hardly know you.'

'Perhaps. But you know all the important things. You know, for a start, that you want to go to bed with me.'

Carly turned swiftly to deny it, but her eyes were caught by his lean, muscular body and the words died in her throat.

'Thank you,' he said softly.

'For—for what?'

'For not lying to me again. Or to yourself.'

Biting her lip, she quickly looked away. 'I wish you'd never come here, Kyle,' she burst out bitterly.

'Does that mean that you want me to leave?'

'Yes.' She said it unhesitatingly.

Coming up behind her, he put his hands on her shoulders and gently turned her to face him. 'Can you look at me and say that?'

Carly's eyes met his, then she shook her head. 'No.' His hands were still on her shoulders and she was very close to him, their bodies only a few tantalising inches apart. He could have easily pulled her to him, but he didn't, and the need to close the gap between them, to step into his arms and feel the strength and warmth of his body envelop her, grew with every second until it threatened to overwhelm her. But somehow she managed to resist, to stand rigidly as the tension grew between them and became electric.

'Come back with me, Carly. You know you want to,' Kyle said at last, his voice harsh, his fingers gripping her shoulders.

'No, I can't. I belong to Andrew and I won't betray him.'

'Why?' he demanded curtly. 'What has he done to make you so loyal to him? Surely it's not because you won't break a promise?'

'Oh, no. It's much, much more than that.' She stepped away from him, unable to think clearly when she was so near. 'My mother died when I was small and then my father was killed in an accident when he was working for Andrew. I didn't have anyone else and I would have been sent to an orphanage, but Andrew and his mother—well, they sort of took me in. They paid for me to go to a good school and I often went to stay with them for holidays. They're all I have. They—they became my family.'

Kyle was looking at her grimly. 'So when Andrew decided he wanted a wife half his age, you accepted.'

'That isn't it at all,' she snapped.

'All right, to make you a closer member of the family, then. Didn't it occur to you that you might fall in love one day?'

'I love Andrew. And I—I want to belong.'

'Of course you love him. You love him like a father. You don't use the word adopted; why didn't he or his mother officially adopt you and make you a real member of their family instead of keeping you as an outsider?'

'I don't know. I . . .'

'Maybe they just wanted to see how you'd turn out first. To make sure they hadn't taken a cuckoo into their luxurious nest,' he interrupted forcefully.

Carly's face had gone very pale. 'You don't have to insult them. They've done nothing to you.'

'No, but they've . . .' He bit off what he was going to say. Instead, earnestly, 'Can't you see that all you feel for him is gratitude?'

She surprised him by saying steadily, 'Yes, I know that; I shall never be able to repay Andrew for what he's done for me. But that isn't all I feel. I was very happy until . . .'

'Until I came along?'

'Yes.' She nodded reluctantly.

'And hasn't that taught you anything, Carly?'

'Yes,' she answered, deliberately being flippant. 'It's taught me never to catch ropes for sailors who are in distress.'

It made Kyle angry. He strode over to her and caught her arm, swinging her round to face him. 'Why won't you face it?' he demanded curtly. 'You're simply trying to fight the fact that you're in love with me out of misplaced loyalty. In five years' time you and Andrew will have nothing in common. You'll either have split up or be staying together just to keep up appearances. You certainly won't be doing him any favour by marrying him when you don't love him,' he finished vehemently.

'Well, that's where you're wrong. I'll marry Andrew and I'll stay with him because he needs me. And don't say that you need me,' she added as Kyle opened his mouth to interrupt, 'because I won't believe you. You're self-sufficient, Kyle. You can get a girl whenever you want one. If I left Andrew for you, we'd probably spend a few months aimlessly drifting along together until you grew tired of me. And then I'd be left with nothing—and no one. I—I couldn't bear that. And there's no way I'm going to hurt Andrew. He's been too good and kind for me ever to do that.'

'And the way you feel about me? Does that count for nothing?'

Carly's hands began to tremble. 'I can't let it.'

'But I can make you.' He put his hands on her wrists and pulled her roughly to him. 'I can kiss you and touch you until your emotions are so aroused that you'll beg me to lay you down on the grass here and make love to you,' he said savagely.

Her heart pounding, Carly took a deep breath before she could speak. 'But you won't.'

After a moment his hands loosened and he stepped back. 'No,' he agreed, 'I won't. Because there's still time for you to come to your senses and come to me of your own accord. And you will. We want each other too much for this to end without our making love.'

'I won't cheat on Andrew,' she insisted stubbornly.

Kyle's brows drew into a frown. 'I've never asked you to—only to give him up.'

'Only!' Carly shook her head in despair. 'Please leave here, Kyle. If you care about me at all, then please go away and leave me in peace.' But he merely shook his head, so that she stamped her foot and exclaimed, 'Oh, for heaven's sake! Don't you ever take no for an answer?'

He grinned suddenly, dispelling the tension. 'Not from anyone who makes me feel the way you do. Especially when they walk and talk and look like you. You've been causing me too many sleepless nights for me ever to let you go.'

'Ever?' She raised her eyebrows.

'Ever,' he agreed steadily, but she didn't believe him.

Taking her arm, he tucked it into his as they retraced their steps through the castle grounds. They had talked themselves into an impasse and there was nothing more to say. Carly glanced up at the moon; it was beginning to wane. Soon the midsummer moon would be past and she would be free of this madness and safely married to Andrew.

Kyle, as if reading her thoughts, said, 'There's still time, Carly. Plenty of time.'

She began to deny it, then stopped in dismay. 'They've closed the gates! We're locked in.'

'What?' Kyle looked to where the tall ornate iron gates were firmly shut across the only exit from the park. He began to laugh. 'Well, well. It looks as if we're going to have to spend the night here together. How opportune!'

'Opportune nothing! And stop laughing, you big ape. I bet you knew they locked these gates at night and brought me in here on purpose.'

'I didn't—I swear it. Ouch!' Still laughing, he lifted his arms in mock self-defence as she punched him.

'Don't just stand there, get us out of here,' she demanded angrily.

'Are you sure you want to? After all, this could be fate, kismet. We could be *meant* to spend the night together.'

'For heaven's sake!' But Carly had a keen sense of the ridiculous and couldn't be angry any longer. She, too, started to laugh. 'What are we going to do? Those gates must be ten feet high. Can you climb over, do you think?'

Kyle shook his head. 'I might be able to, but I don't think you'd make it. We'd better look round and see if there's an easier place.'

They explored almost the whole circuit of the park before they at last found a tree that grew near the high wall that surrounded it, and which Carly thought she could climb.

'I'll help you.' Kyle went first and gave her a hand up the most difficult bits, telling her where to put her feet.

Leaves and bits of twig caught in her hair and once a piece of branch got caught in the front of her shirt and tore the thin material, but Carly was concentrating on keeping her balance and didn't take any notice.

'Okay?' Kyle got on to the top of the wall and sat astride it, reaching dangerously down to help her to do the same.

'Yes.' She was breathless and hanging on to him

tightly. The ground seemed an awfully long way down. 'What do we do now?'

'I'm going to jump. Then I'll catch you when you jump. Okay?'

Carly gulped and nodded, letting him go and clinging to the wall instead.

'Good girl!' Leaning forward, he kissed her until she gasped for breath, unable to leave go to push him away.

'You idiot! We must look like a pair of cats up here.'

He grinned and swung a leg over the wall. 'I'd fight all the other tomcats for you any day!' Then he jumped, landing with a thud on the hard ground below. 'Come on,' he called, his voice lowered.

'Kyle, I'm—I'm scared.' Carly gripped the wall, feeling its hard grittiness digging into her palms.

'I'll catch you; there's nothing to be afraid of.' But she still hesitated until he called, 'Trust me, sweetheart. I won't let you get hurt.' Then she swung her leg over the wall, let go, and jumped.

Kyle caught her easily and lowered her to her feet, but kept his arms round her. Her hands were on his shoulders and she didn't attempt to draw away. 'So you do trust me?' he said softly.

She smiled rather tremulously, her heart beating fast—with fear still, she told herself. 'So it would seem.'

'Good. Maybe I'm making progress with you after all.' And he kissed her warmly, raising his head at length to say reluctantly, 'I hate to break this up, but I think we landed in someone's garden and it might be a good idea to get out of here before we're accused of burglary.'

Taking her hand, Kyle led the way as they pushed their way through a shrubbery on to a lawn at the back of a large house. They ran across it and crept by the house itself, which was all in darkness. Somewhere nearby a dog began to bark and they froze, but then Carly started to giggle helplessly and Kyle had to put his hand over her mouth until the dog's owner shouted at it and it stopped with a howl, then they hastily ran down the driveway and let themselves out of the front gate, taking to their heels until they had turned the corner.

Carly stopped, out of breath and doubled up with laughter. 'Oh, lor! When that dog barked I nearly died; I really felt like a criminal!'

'I thought for sure you'd give us away when you started to laugh. But I had a hell of a job stopping myself.' He grinned down at her. 'You're crazy, do you know that?'

'I'm crazy! What about you? If it had been Andrew he'd have attracted someone's attention and made them find the official to come and unlock the gates. He'd never have climbed over and ended up in someone's back garden.'

'No, but then Andrew would never have taken you in the park and got locked in in the first place, would he?' Kyle pointed out.

'I suppose not,' Carly agreed, sobering.

But he soon had her laughing again as he took her hand and said, 'I hope you know where we are, because I'm utterly lost. We might just have to wander around all night.'

'No such luck, I know exactly where we are. This way.'

They walked back towards the Mews and near it saw a policeman on his beat, and Carly felt so guilty that she hid in Kyle's big shadow. They were both still laughing about it as they reached her flat. Carly got out her key and turned to say goodnight, but Kyle put his hands on her waist and drew her towards him.

'Take your filthy hands off her!'

The peremptory command came out of the darkness

and Carly whirled round in horror as Andrew stepped angrily out of the shadows towards them. Kyle didn't seem at all surprised and, of course, took no notice, keeping his hands firmly where they were. But Carly quickly tried to step away from him, frightened by the situation and the look of fury on Andrew's face.

'You heard me,' he barked. 'Keep away from her!'

'Andrew, please,' Carly began nervously, but he caught hold of her arm and pulled her roughly away from Kyle.

'I have a few things to say to you,' he announced grimly.

'Yes, all right.' She turned the key in the lock, acutely aware that there were still lights on in the mews and that people were probably listening and watching them.

Andrew pushed her inside and tried to slam the door in Kyle's face, but Kyle put his foot in the way and shouldered his way in. 'Get out of here, you lout!' Andrew was so angry that he didn't even care that Kyle was a good deal bigger than he was.

'I'm staying,' answered Kyle, his face determined.

'No, please. I'll be all right,' Carly assured him.

'Are you crazy? I'm not leaving you alone with him. The mood he's in, he could hurt you.'

'No, he won't. Please, Kyle, you're only making it worse.' She looked up at him pleadingly. 'Just leave us alone. Please.' At last he nodded reluctantly.

'Okay, but I'll wait outside. Yell if you need me.'

'All right.'

Kyle stopped her from shutting the door and watched as she went up the stairs to where Andrew was waiting for her. As soon as she entered the room, he slammed the door shut. He was quivering with anger, his hands balled into tight fists. Carly had never seen him so angry, and her heart sank. 'Andrew, I . . .'

'Don't give me any damn excuses; I don't want to hear them. I came back here because I regretted that we'd argued and wanted to make it up, and you weren't here. So I waited for you. *For hours*. And you turn up with that—that bearded hippie! After I expressly asked you never to see him again. You just went straight to him!'

'No, I didn't. I went out for a meal with some friends and he happened to come into the restaurant.'

'Do you expect me to believe that when I see you alone with him, laughing together and him putting his arms round you?' he demanded furiously. 'What the hell are you trying to do—make me the laughing stock of the whole town?'

Her face pale, Carly said steadily, 'That's the last thing I'd ever want to do. I know how much your reputation in the town means to you. But don't worry, you'll still get to be the Mayor one day,' she added with a touch of sarcasm.

But he didn't even notice. 'I've been waiting for you for nearly three hours. Where have you been with him? On his damn boat, I suppose.'

Carly looked at him quickly, realising that he must have been making enquiries about Kyle to learn that he lived on the boat. 'No,' she answered as calmly as she could, 'I haven't been on his boat with him.' She hoped that by being calm she might lessen his fury, but it seemed to have the reverse effect.

'But you admit that you've been with him. And don't say that you haven't. Look at you!' he spun her round to face the mirror. 'Your clothes are torn and there are twigs and leaves in your hair. What did he do, throw you down on the grass?'

'Andrew, please listen to me. It wasn't like that,' Carly said desperately, completely dismayed by her appearance and realising how it must seem to him. 'I know it looks bad, but I can explain.'

'I don't want to hear it,' he shouted. 'And don't try to tell me that you've never been in his boat, because you were seen leaving it at some ungodly hour of the morning—over two weeks ago!'

Her night of midsummer madness; Carly wished now with all her heart that it had never happened. 'Yes,' she began, 'I did go on his boat with him one night, but . . .'

'Then you admit you spent the night with him?' Andrew's face was bright red with rage.

'*No!* Not in the way you mean. I've never . . .'

But she had no time to say it before he caught hold of her arms, hurting her in his fury. 'Tell me the truth, damn you! Have you been to bed with him? Have you?'

But before Carly could voice her hot denial, Kyle erupted into the room, crashing the door back on its hinges as he ran across to take hold of Andrew from behind, pinning his arms to his sides and lifting him bodily away from her. 'Are you all right?' he demanded urgently. 'I could hear him shouting at you down in the street!'

'Yes, I'm okay.' Automatically she rubbed her arms where Andrew's fingers had dug into her. 'Let him go. Please,' she added, seeing that Kyle was still holding him.

He did so, reluctantly, but his intervention seemed to have jolted Andrew out of his rage. His face was white and he was shaking, but striving hard to control it. 'Get out of here,' he grated, using the authoritarian manner Carly had sometimes heard him use to his employees. 'This is nothing to do with you.'

'It seems to be everything to do with me,' Kyle contradicted. 'And I'm not leaving.' Folding his arms, he leaned against the wall, looking tall and menacing, ready to move into action again if the need arose.

His declaration seemed to create an impasse. Carly went over to the door and shut it, then crossed to draw the curtains; if the neighbours could hear at least she wouldn't let them see what was going on as well.

Gathering the shattered remnants of his dignity, Andrew drew himself up and said coldly, 'I wish to talk to my fiancée alone.'

'No way.' Kyle stood his ground.

Carly, looking at them both glaring at each other, like a pair of boxers sizing each other up in a ring, was suddenly exasperated. 'This is my flat and I'll say who stays or who goes,' she declared angrily. 'And right now I don't find the behaviour of either of you very edifying. If you want to talk to me, Andrew, then I suggest you leave it until you've had time to cool down. I'm sorry if I kept you waiting, but I wasn't to know that you were going to come back here. And anyway, if you'd phoned first you'd have known I was out and saved yourself a lot of unnecessary aggro.'

She had never put Andrew in his place before, and he looked at her in undisguised astonishment. But then she turned on Kyle and her heart skipped a beat as she saw the amused admiration in his blue eyes. 'Atta girl,' he said softly.

She flushed and rounded on him. 'And you're just as bad! I asked you to leave this to me, but you wouldn't listen.'

'I'm not the type who stands back and lets a woman take all the kicks,' he pointed out grimly.

'Andrew's just a little upset, that's all.'

'Humph!' All Kyle's derisive disgust was in that sound.

'Would you mind not talking about me as if I wasn't

here?' the other man broke in. 'And don't try to make excuses for me either; I don't need any. My behaviour is perfectly justified.'

And he was right, Carly admitted to herself. He had every reason to be angry. She hadn't behaved at all well by Andrew. But she had the feeling that now wasn't the time to start admitting that. 'Please,' she said tiredly, 'would you both go home? It's very late.'

Andrew bristled. 'I have no intention of leaving until this is settled once and for all.'

Kyle looked as if he agreed with him and wanted to stay and have it out, but he took one glance at Carly's pale face and sagging shoulders and said decisively, 'Not tonight you won't. You heard what Carly said, she's had enough. We're both leaving.'

For a minute Andrew looked as if he was going to argue, but then something seemed to occur to him and he nodded, straightening his jacket and tie. 'Very well.' He nodded to her curtly. 'Goodnight. I'll see you tomorrow. I'll phone first, of course, to make sure you're at home—alone,' he added as a parting thrust.

'Goodnight, Andrew,' Carly answered dully.

Kyle didn't say anything, he just looked at her steadily, his eyes holding hers, then he nodded and preceded Andrew down the stairs, knowing that the other man wouldn't leave before he did.

Carly shut the sitting-room door behind them and listened to them going down the stairs. She heard Andrew say something and rushed to the window to look out, petrified that they might have a fight or something. The front door closed and the two men came into view. They stopped outside and Andrew seemed to be doing all the talking, using his hands for emphasis. Kyle shook his head at first, then shrugged, and to Carly's astonishment they moved off together, walking side by side down to the entrance to the Mews.

She stared after them, fighting down an urge to run and catch them up, find out what Andrew had been saying, where they were going. When they were out of sight, Carly slowly lowered the curtain and began to move agitatedly around the room wondering what the hell was going on. Oh God, what a mess! She'd never seen Andrew so angry, in fact he'd never once been really angry with her before, not even when she'd done stupid things as a teenager. And it was all her fault, all of it. She should never have allowed herself to get involved with Kyle in the first place. The fact that she was involved brought her up short. Standing in the middle of the room with her arms crossed across her chest, Carly realised for the first time just how much she cared for Kyle. He had described to her what it felt like to be in love, but she had deliberately not applied it to herself, instead attacking Kyle and accusing him of being a womaniser. But now she acknowledged that she was deeply attracted to him, perhaps even in love.

The admission didn't bring her any joy, only heartache. Turning off the lights, Carly went to the window that overlooked the meadows and sat on the wide window sill, her chin resting on her knees, staring out into the moonlit night. The time had come when she had to make a decision: to follow her head or her heart. Only it wasn't as simple as that. When was life ever so clear cut? The love she felt for Kyle and Andrew was completely different, but it was still love and it still went as deep. How could she possibly just throw aside all the years she had known Andrew and all that he had done for her because she was physically in love with Kyle? And how could she deny this overwhelming yearning for Kyle and cold-bloodedly give herself to

Andrew? Which man, which life to choose? Safety and
security with Andrew, or passion and possible
heartbreak with Kyle who was little better than a
vagabond.

She sat there for hours, tortured by doubt and
uncertainty, knowing that whatever decision she made
she must give herself to wholeheartedly, cutting the
other man in her life completely and forever. But
the thought was always at the back of Carly's mind that
the decision might have been made for her; Andrew
might have persuaded Kyle to leave Grantston or, after
seeing her with Kyle tonight, he might have decided
that he no longer wanted to marry her. It was morning
before she moved, cramped and stiff, and at last
undressed and went to bed, but she had made her
decision, the only decision she could make, and was
resolved to carry it through.

Worry about what had happened between the two
men prevented her from sleeping properly; it had been
completely unnatural for them to go off together like
that, and Carly was petrified that they might have got
into a fight or worse; Andrew had been almost out of
his mind with anger. So, when she got up at seven-
thirty, too worried and anxious to stay in bed any
longer, there were dark smudges of tiredness around her
eyes, accentuating the paleness of her face. She was
desperate to know what had happened between them
and longed to contact one of them to find out, but
knew that she couldn't make the first move, she had to
let them come to her.

At nine the phone rang and she snatched up the
receiver eagerly, too nervous to say the number and
stammering out a hello. But it was only one of her
dressmakers with a query over a design. Somehow
Carly managed to put her off and sat on the floor by

the phone, hands shaking, her nerves in shreds. She
tried to occupy herself with her work, but it was
impossible to concentrate and she grew more and more
fidgety as time passed. And angry too; you'd think one
of them would have had the decency to phone and let
her know what had happened!

But when the door bell did ring, it was neither
Andrew nor Kyle, but Mrs Naughton who stood on the
doorstep, smartly dressed in a silk summer suit and
beflowered hat. 'Good morning, Carly. May I come in?'
she asked when Carly just stood staring at her in
consternation.

'Oh, yes. Yes, of course.' Pulling herself together,
Carly led the way upstairs. 'Do sit down. May I get you
a cup of coffee?'

'Thank you, that would be very welcome. It's so hot
again today; I think I'll almost be glad when the weather
breaks,' Mrs Naughton observed, seating herself in an
easy chair, her manner outwardly exactly as normal.

Carly made the coffee, her hands fumbling, remembering to use her china cups because Mrs
Naughton didn't like drinking out of mugs, and then
carrying them into the sitting-room on a tray.

'Thank you, my dear.' The older woman stirred in
milk and looked at Carly narrowly. 'You look tired.'

'Yes. I—I didn't sleep very well last night.' Carly
took her own cup and crossed to sit on the settee. She
took a sip, then put the cup aside, unable to drink it.
'Did Andrew ask you to come?'

'Yes. He told me what happened last night and he
thought it might help if we had a chat about things.'

'What things? What did he tell you?' Carly demanded
abruptly.

Mrs Naughton's brows rose slightly at her tone.
'He merely told me that he'd called round to see you

and found that you'd been with another man. Isn't that so?'

Put like that it sounded starkly cheap and contemptible, although Carly was pretty sure that Mrs Naughton didn't realise the commoner meaning of the phrase she'd used. Biting her lip, she answered, 'Something like that.'

'You must forgive me if I sound old-fashioned, Carly, but it's hardly what one expects of a girl who is about to be married in only a few weeks' time. And especially not what I expected of you.' She waited, but when Carly didn't speak, went on, 'I need hardly tell you that this has been a great blow to Andrew. He was terribly upset when he got home last night. I've seldom seen him in such a state. And naturally he wants to know where he stands. Just how—involved you are with this other man.'

At first Carly had felt much as she had at shool when the headmistress had sent for her to discipline her over some misdemeanour, but then the incongruity of sitting here, calmly discussing her feelings over cups of coffee struck her and she remembered that she wasn't a schoolgirl any more. 'If Andrew wants to know that, then I think he should ask me himself,' she said sharply. 'After all, this is between him and me.'

Setting down her cup, Mrs Naughton said smoothly, 'Of course. But as you're so young and have no one of your own, he thought you might be in need of another woman to talk things over with. And don't forget, my dear, that it's my family you are marrying into. As Andrew's wife and my daughter-in-law you will hold a very privileged position in Grantston. One that can be very fulfilling and extremely rewarding, if you'll let it.'

'Yes, I'm quite aware of the position I'll hold. Andrew has told me about it—often.'

'Because he's worked hard and it means a lot to him. Just as you do, Carly. Make no mistake; Andrew may not be very demonstrative, but he cares for you very deeply.'

'Yes, I know.' Agitatedly she stood up and moved to the window, looking blindly down into the mews.

'Do you want to talk it over?'

Carly shook her head. 'No.'

Mrs Naughton's voice hardened. 'You realise that you have to make a decision. Andrew will not tolerate this situation any longer.'

Turning to face her, Carly, her face very pale, said, 'Yes, I know.'

'And,' her nose wrinkled in distaste, 'this kind of thing must not happen again, now—or ever.'

'I know that, too.'

'Very well.' Mrs Naughton got to her feet, picked up her bag and gloves and looked at Carly expectantly. 'I'll leave you to think over what I've said.'

'That won't be necessary,' Carly replied as steadily as she could. 'My mind was already made up before you came.'

'Good. I'm glad to hear it. What have you decided? To be sensible, I hope.'

Carly's chin came up. 'I prefer to tell Andrew myself.'

For a moment a frown of annoyance creased the other woman's brow, but then she gave a slight shrug. 'Very well, if that's what you want. There is, however, one question that Andrew demands an answer to; have you or have you not slept with this man?'

For a moment rage surged through her, but went as quickly as it came. 'No,' she answered dully, 'I haven't.'

The older woman nodded without comment. 'I expect Andrew will call round after dinner this evening.'

'He went to work?'

Mrs Naughton looked at her in surprise. 'Yes, of course he went to work.' She said it as if Carly was a naughty child whose affairs were of little real importance.

Feeling as if she'd been put firmly in her place, she showed the older woman out and went back to wait. Unable to understand why Kyle didn't come to the flat or at least telephone, Carly could only assume that it had something to do with the two men going off together last night. There seemed to be no other reason to explain his silence, although she couldn't really believe that Kyle would willingly stay away.

It was eight-thirty before Andrew came, on what had been the longest day in her life. He looked at her narrowly as he came into the room, dressed in a sports jacket and trousers, his brown hair neatly brushed, his face outwardly calm; a far cry from his wild anger of last night. But he didn't kiss her in greeting as he usually did.

'Mother told me that she called on you this morning, but you refused to confide in her,' he began abruptly.

Carly wouldn't have put it as bluntly as that, but she merely nodded silently.

Andrew looked at her frowningly, wanting her to take the initiative, running an agitated hand through his hair when she stayed silent, his other hand balled into a tight fist as he strove to control his emotions. 'Well?' he demanded. 'What are you going to do?'

CHAPTER SEVEN

In a flat empty voice, Carly answered, 'Marry you—if you still want me to.'

Andrew's hand slowly relaxed. 'And you'll agree never to see this Anderson fellow again?' he questioned harshly. She nodded, but he said, 'I want your solemn promise.'

'All right, I promise. I won't see him again.'

He looked at her searchingly, but Carly met his eyes quite openly and he nodded in satisfaction. 'So nothing's changed.'

'No,' Carly agreed dully, 'nothing's changed.'

'Very well, then. The wedding will go ahead as we planned.' He came over to her, able to be a little magnanimous now that he was sure he'd won. Taking her hand, he said, 'You mustn't feel too badly, darling. You're young and innocent and that—that damned rogue tried to take advantage of you. But I understand, and I forgive you. Although I must admit that I was more than a little upset and angry last night.' He gave an unsteady laugh. 'For a while I was afraid I was going to lose you.'

'You needn't have been. I always said that I wanted to go ahead and marry you.'

'So you did. But you seemed to be more than a little attached to the fellow.'

Carly drew her hand away. 'I've said I won't see him again; do we have to discuss it?' She went across the room and turned on a lamp to dispel the shadows that had started to darken the corners of the room.

'Not if you don't want to. I'll go to his boat tonight and tell him to clear out, that you want nothing more to do with him.'

'But I must tell him that myself! I can't let you . . .'

'No, you damn well won't,' Andrew interrupted with immediate violence. 'You've just promised you'll never see him again.'

'Only to tell him. To say goodbye,' Carly protested.

'No. I don't trust that ba . . .' He bit off the expletive. 'You can write and tell him. And I'll take the letter.'

'But . . .' she started to protest again, then shrugged tiredly. 'All right.' Moving across to the chest of drawers, she took out a pen and writing paper, then sat down at the table.

Andrew came up behind her. 'And I want to see the letter,' he said grimly.

For a moment Carly's knuckles showed white as she gripped the pen, but then she began to write, although her hand was shaking so much that the words were unsteady. The message was very simple and very final. 'Kyle, I am going ahead with my marriage to Andrew. I don't want to see you again. Carly.'

Andrew had been reading over her shoulder and when she'd done she simply got up and moved away, leaving him to put the letter in an envelope and slip it into his pocket. 'I'll give it to him on my way home tonight.'

He looked at her as she stood with her back to him, head bowed, then he came over and turned her to face him, his hands on her arms. His voice harsh, he said, 'Was it the truth you told my mother this morning?'

Carly didn't have to ask him what about. Two bright patches of colour came into her cheeks as she replied stiffly, 'I don't lie, Andrew.'

'No. No, at least you've never lied to me.' His hands

trembling slightly, he pulled her to him and began to kiss her.

For a few seconds she resisted, standing rigidly in his arms, her eyes tightly closed, but then Carly forced herself to relax, to open her mouth and submit to his embrace. Pulling down the sun-top she was wearing, Andrew's hands went to her breasts, squeezing and fondling, so much that he hurt her and left red marks on her skin, but she made no sound of protest.

'You realise,' he said thickly, 'that there's no question now of waiting till the wedding. I'm not going to run the risk of losing you to someone else again.'

Carly nodded, unable to speak, and he led her into her bedroom, making her lie down while he took off most of his own clothes. Then he came and lay down beside her, kissing her again as he took off her top and skirt so that she was wearing nothing but a pair of panties. Andrew was forty-three years old and she knew that there had been several women in his life, so he wasn't exactly inexperienced. Before, when he had caressed and fondled her, she had enjoyed the pleasant sensations it had aroused in her, but he had always been careful never to go too far or to do anything she might object to. But tonight he didn't seem to care. He seemed determined to make her prove that she had submitted completely to his will, touching her wherever he wanted and making her put her hands on him and then telling her what he wanted her to do to give him pleasure.

His voice grew hoarse and his hands left bruise marks on her skin, but she did what he wanted. She knew that he was going to take her and she steeled herself to accept what was going to happen. She'd made her choice and there was no backing out now. When they were married this would happen all the time. There was nothing to be afraid of. Even if that ecstatic, wonderful frenzy of desire and need wasn't there, there was nothing to be afraid of.

Andrew's body was dripping with perspiration and she could feel his heart thumping as he half lay on top of her, kissing her with avid passion, his fingers making her body jerk as he explored her. Then, dimly, she heard the phone start to ring in the other room. She made an involuntary movement, and it was only then that Andrew heard it. He swore and caught hold of her. 'No, let it ring.'

'But it could be important.'

'I don't care. Forget it.' He kissed her again, but the phone went on ringing and it was impossible to completely ignore it, even though Andrew tried. Neither of them said it, but both of them were more than aware that it could be Kyle who was calling. It seemed to go on interminably, but at last the ringing stopped. Andrew gave a grunt of satisfaction and began to make love to her again. But five minutes later the imperative buzz of the door bell filled the flat, followed by a loud, hammering knock on the door.

'God damn him to hell!' Andrew swore in furious frustration. 'He promised to . . .' He broke off and rolled off the bed, began to put on his clothes.

'What? What did Kyle promise?' Carly sat up, pulling the duvet over her nakedness.

'Eh? Oh, nothing.' He zipped up his trousers and went into the sitting-room to look out of the open window.

Hastily she pulled on her clothes and followed him. 'I want to know what happened between you two last night. What did you make him promise?'

'I've told you, nothing. I'm going to put paid to that devil once and for all!' Picking up the phone, he began to dial.

'What are you doing? Andrew, what promise did he make?' Agitatedly she pulled at his sleeve.

'It's nothing to do with you. Go and pack; I'm taking you home with me.'

'But I don't want to go. Your mother . . .'

'Do you think I'm going to leave you here in reach of that damned hippie?' He turned away as someone spoke to him on the phone. 'Yes. I'd like to report a disturbance. A man is trying to force his way into one of the flats in the mews at the back of the High Street. Yes, that's right. No, I don't wish to give my name, but please send someone here as soon as possible.' Then he put down the receiver.

Carly stared at him aghast. 'You reported him to the police!'

'It's no more than he deserves,' Andrew said shortly, but added, 'Don't worry, I don't want a scandal any more than you do. The police will only move him on—unless he cuts up rough and tries to fight them off.'

Her face pale, she said, 'Kyle would never hurt anyone for no reason.'

Andrew glanced at her, then said sharply, 'Go and pack some clothes.'

'Not until you tell me what went on between you last night,' she said stubbornly, standing her ground.

For a moment, he glared at her angrily, then shrugged. 'All right, if you really must have it. Your precious hippie friend demanded money from me in return for keeping away from you. At first I refused, but then he began to make threats—disgusting threats—so I gave him two hundred pounds on his promise to leave Grantston immediately.'

Carly gripped the table edge tightly. 'What threats?'

'Do I have to spell it out to you? Not that his word is to be trusted. This demonstration is obviously in the hope of getting more money out of me. Well, this time he's going to be disappointed!'

The hammering on the front door ceased suddenly and there was the sound of voices outside. Andrew went to the window to watch, careful to stand back out of sight. Carly hardly heard and she certainly didn't want to see; she felt physically sick inside and went back into the bedroom to sit on the edge of the bed, her head in her hands. When all was quiet again, Andrew came to stand in the doorway. Without speaking, Carly got up and took her suitcase from the wardrobe, began to pack some clothes.

Fortunately Mrs Naughton was out at a committee meeting when they got to The Elms, so Carly was spared having to face her and explain why she was there.

'I'd like to go straight up to my room, if you don't mind, Andrew.'

'Yes, of course. The guest room should be made up.' Andrew led the way to the pretty room at the back of the house that she had always slept in when she had stayed here before. 'I'll leave you to unpack. Would you like any supper or anything?'

'No. No, thank you. I'd just like to go to bed.' She stood there in the middle of the room, waiting for him to go.

'All right. I'll tell Mother you're here.' He hesitated awkwardly, then came over and would have kissed her, but saw her set face and changed his mind. 'You've done the sensible thing,' he said rather shortly. 'In a couple of weeks all this will be forgotten.'

Carly nodded and tried to smile, too choked up to speak, but he seemed satisfied and at last left her alone.

For the second night running, Carly didn't sleep; she heard Mrs Naughton's car drive up and could imagine her and Andrew talking over what had happened, although the house was too big to actually hear. But an hour or so later she did hear them coming up to bed and saying goodnight. After that she lay for a long time in fear that Andrew would come to her room and want to make love to her, to carry on from where he had been so prematurely interrupted. But as the hours passed and he didn't come, Carly slowly began to relax and her brain to function again as she realised that he was probably too fastidious to take her when his mother was in the house. She gave a small sigh of relief and her mind immediately filled with thoughts of Kyle, thoughts that she'd been trying hard to fight away from, but now his deceit and betrayal tore at her heart, and she turned her face into the pillow and cried helplessly. It had been lies, nothing but lies, he had used her just to extort money out of Andrew, and like a fool she'd believed that he really cared.

The next day she got up early, made her bed and tidied her room before she went down to breakfast, a habit Mrs Naughton had instilled into her when she had first come to stay there as a child. At breakfast she conversed politely with Andrew and his mother, answering whenever they spoke to her, but she made no attempt to say anything for herself and there was a tight, dead look to her usually animated features. The subject that was uppermost in all their minds was carefully avoided, and when Andrew had gone to his office, Carly obediently fell in with Mrs Naughton's suggestion that she start writing thank-you letters for the wedding presents that had already arrived. It was obviously the older woman's intention to keep her busy, and Carly had no quibble with that—she was grateful for anything that would pass the time.

The telephone rang several times during the

morning for Mrs Naughton, either friends or to do with her charity work, but once Carly noticed a new note in her voice as she answered it. 'No, you cannot,' the other woman said stiffly. 'Certainly not! Miss Morgan has nothing whatever to say to you. Don't ring this number again.' And she abruptly replaced the receiver. Looking up, she met Carly's eyes, dark in her pale face, and the two women stared at each other as the phone immediately began to ring again. Deliberately Mrs Naughton reached out, took the phone off the hook and laid it down on the desk in front of her, then she calmly went on with the speech she was preparing. After a long moment, Carly too turned back to the letter she was writing, trying desperately to ignore the faint but insistent voice that eventually gave up.

They never left her alone in the house. If Mrs Naughton had to go out during the day she insisted on taking Carly with her unless Andrew was there. The weather was very hot and sultry, so Carly spent most of the time in the garden, using the excuse of sunbathing to just lie there, no longer even able to find any enthusiasm for her work. When Andrew was at home she tried to put on a bright front, but it didn't deceive anyone, and she was aware that he and his mother were constantly watching her, so that she was glad to escape and be alone. In the evenings Andrew insisted on taking her out, to the Golf Club and to a restaurant patronised by a great many people they knew, to 'kill any gossip', as he put it.

On the third morning she was there the housekeeper came out into the garden to tell her that there was a phone call for her. 'Is it a man?' Mrs Naughton demanded from her seat in the shade of one of the elm trees.

'No, madam, it's a shop in Bristol with a query about an order.'

'Oh, very well.' The older woman nodded consent.

'Hallo. Carly Morgan here.' Carly picked up the phone in Andrew's study, wondering how the shop had known where to find her.

'Hi. It's Alison. There's someone here who wants to speak to you.'

Before Carly could gather her wits and realise the trick they'd played, Kyle's voice came on the line and her heart did a crazy somersault so that she could hardly breathe. 'Carly? Sweetheart? What the hell did he do to you to make you send me that letter?' he demanded brusquely. 'Did he force you to write it? Or did he write it himself? Carly? Are you still there?'

Somehow she managed to find her voice and say unsteadily, 'Yes, I'm—I'm here.'

'Are you all right? Has he hurt you?' His tone was sharp, anxious.

'No, I'm all right.' She knew that she ought to slam down the receiver and refuse to speak to him, but it was impossible. Her heart was filled with pain and she gripped the receiver tightly in both hands.

'And that damned letter? How did he make you . . .'

'He didn't make me,' Carly broke in, the hurt turning to sudden anger. 'I wanted to write it. And I meant what I said. I meant it even before Andrew told me what you'd done, what you were.' Her voice faltered as she bit back a sob, then rushed on, 'Go away from here! Leave me alone. I hate you for what you did. I hate you!'

'What do you mean? What did he tell you I did? Carly . . .'

But she put the receiver down on his protests, held it down as if by doing so she could push him out of her life. The phone rang again at once, but she didn't answer it, merely walked out of the room and left it ringing, telling the housekeeper on the way that she wasn't in to any more calls. But, unable to face Mrs Naughton's questions, intead of going back into the garden Carly went upstairs to her room and lay down on the bed for a long time, gazing up at the ceiling, wondering why Kyle hadn't left Grantston, if he really thought that by hounding her he could get more money out of Andrew. She tried to pull herself together, realising that she'd had a lucky escape; she could have so easily given herself to Kyle; let physical attraction overcome her common sense. Then she would probably have lost everything. At least she still had her future with Andrew, and she had learnt the bitter lesson of never trusting a stranger. One she would never forget.

Eventually work intruded itself whether she liked it or not, and Carly had to go to one of her dressmakers to pick up a consignment of clothes and take them to a shop in Bath, Mrs Naughton coming with her 'for the ride', as she expressed her excuse. But the next time the older woman had a committee meeting she couldn't get out of, so Carly was reluctantly allowed to go alone. After all, they couldn't guard her for ever.

The sun had been shining on to the Mini and it was like an oven, the plastic upholstery burning into her legs below the turned-up blue shorts she wore with just a sun-top and a wide leather belt. Carly opened all the windows and welcomed the breeze as she drove along to see her other dressmaker. She was there for about an hour, paying the woman for the work she had done and talking over any probems.

She came out of the dressmaker's house carrying an armful of clothes in their plastic bags and had to balance them on her knee as she juggled with keys and handbag.

'Here, let me help you.' A hand appeared out of nowhere and took the keys from her to open the door of the car, then took the clothes from her lifeless arms and tossed them on to the back seats.

Carly stood completely still, unable to move, as she looked up into Kyle's face. His blue eyes were fixed on her, devouring each feature, the unhappiness in her mouth, the shadows round her lifeless eyes. 'What the hell has he done to you?' he demanded savagely.

She moved then and tried to get into the car, but he slammed the door shut and caught her wrist, pulling her round to face him so that she was leaning against the car, powerless to move away, her body trembling convulsively.

'Carly, my darling girl, what is it? What has he . . .'

'Don't! Don't call me that.' She wrenched her wrist free, but Kyle immediately put his hands against the car on either side of her so that she was still a prisoner.

'Why not? Why shouldn't I say what I feel?'

His eyes were on her face intently, but she turned her head away, unable to look at him. 'Because you don't mean it. You never have. You were just using me.' Again she tried to get into the car but he pulled her back. 'Don't touch me!' Her voice rose agitatedly as she brought up her hands in a futile attempt to defend herself. 'I can't bear it when you touch me!'

'Can't you?' His grip tightened on her arms. 'Or is it just that you can't bear what I make you feel?' His voice hardened. 'I don't know what Naughton told you about me, Carly, but you must know it isn't true. This is the truth, and only this matters.'

He pulled her into his arms, drowning her protests with his mouth as he kissed her. Carly tried to fight, tried desperately, but her hands were pinned against his chest and when she tried to turn her head away he put a hand in her hair and held her a captive to the onslaught on her mouth. She grew rigid then, determined to resist as he sought to make her respond. His lips were hard against hers, seeking, probing, but still she resisted him. He grew angry then, she could feel it as his body tensed, his heartbeat increasing under her hand. His grip tightened and he drew her closer. Carly tried to pull away, but the roof of the car was pressing painfully into her back. So there was nothing she could do but stand and try to bear it as his mouth took hers in dominating, hungry passion.

The world began to whirl around her and she couldn't fight it any more. She moaned against his mouth and her body shuddered convulsively. The fires that she had tried so hard to suppress burst into flaming life, consuming her senses until she knew she couldn't resist any longer. She made small, agonised sounds and tears began to flood down her cheeks.

Kyle felt them and lifted his head, his eyes staring into hers. 'Oh, God, don't cry. Please don't cry, my love.'

He lifted a hand to clumsily try to wipe away her tears, but Carly shook her head and tried to push his hand away. 'Don't! Leave me alone! Oh, why can't you leave me alone?'

His face grew grim and he was about to reply when a high female voice intruded. 'Carly? Are you all right? Is this man bothering you?'

Turning her head, Carly saw that it was her dressmaker, who must have seen what was going on from the house and had come out to offer assistance, half afraid but very determined and armed with a rolling-pin that would be as effective against Kyle as one of the dressmaking pins stuck into the front of her apron. She would have looked ludicrous if she hadn't been so gallant; she was only a small woman and Kyle was almost twice her size.

'Yes. Yes, he is.' Taking advantage of Kyle's surprise, Carly slipped into her car and slammed the door, then started the engine.

'Carly, wait!' Kyle grabbed hold of the door and pulled it open, but she had the car in gear now and began to pull away, putting her foot on the accelerator. 'Stay here. Let me talk to you!' Kyle yelled, hanging on to the car and running along beside it, bent double because it was so low.

'Go away!' she shouted at him. 'Leave me alone!' With a sob she changed into a higher gear and increased the speed.

Kyle swore and desperately tried to reach into the car to switch off the engine, but Carly beat at his hand and pushed the accelerator down as hard as she could. For a few minutes he hung on grimly, but suddenly he wasn't there any more and she leaned out of the car and caught the flying door, slamming it shut. When she looked in the rear mirror Kyle was sprawled in the road and her heart gave a sudden jerk of fear. Almost she slowed down and would have stopped, but then she saw him pick himself up, look round and begin to limp after her, so she hastily picked up speed again and left him behind.

When she got back to The Elms later that day, Carly said nothing about what had happened. If they heard about it from some other source it would be just too bad, there was no way she could tell them and answer their questions, listen to their comments.

It was a Friday, and Andrew came home early and told his mother off for using a sprinkler on the lawn when there was a water shortage and a ban on using garden hoses.

'Nonsense,' Mrs Naughton returned. 'That doesn't apply to us. Why, the head of the Water Company is a friend of mine. We often play bridge together. And anyway, we have to keep the garden looking nice for the wedding. It's less than a month away now.'

'Personally I think the weather will break before long. It can't go on much longer,' Andrew remarked, going over to the open windows and looking up into the cloudless sky. 'I'll be glad to have an end to this damned heat. It's causing havoc in the factory. The men threatened to walk out because it was too hot to work. I had to hire a whole lorry-load of air-conditioning units to keep them happy.'

There was an official reception at the Town Hall that night, during which Carly tried hard to appear bright and happy, even if she didn't feel it. Many of the people there were coming to the wedding and when the men had gone off to the bar as they usually did, nearly all the women asked her about it, wanting to know details of her dress, the ceremony, the reception, her honeymoon; there seemed to be nothing they didn't want to know about. That their interest was mostly kind and friendly, Carly knew, and she tried her best to be civil, but by the end of the evening she felt that if she was asked just one more question she'd scream.

It was midnight before they got home and Mrs Naughton had gone to bed. As he had for the last few nights, Andrew took her out into the garden where they couldn't be seen by anyone happening to look out from the house, and began to make love to her. He used her as he had that night at the flat, but stopped short of going the whole way. Carly leant against a tree, unresisting. She wasn't impervious to what he was doing to her and he liked her to react, to catch her breath when he touched her in a sensitive place and to gasp or give a little cry when he hurt her. He seemed to hurt her more than he used to, and now he didn't care so much, didn't apologise. He grew very hot and passionate, his voice hoarse. 'Tomorrow,' he said thickly. 'Tomorrow we'll go to your flat and make love properly.'

Carly quivered, but said, 'All right, if that's what you want.'

'I want you. I want to . . .' He went on to tell her just how he wanted her, and Carly stifled a tremor of revulsion; Andrew had never been like this before, it had never even occurred to her that he could be like it.

But he would change she told herself as she undressed and got ready for bed, when they were married he would get over this and be his kind and considerate self again, as he had always been. Turning out the light, she went over to the window and pushed it open as far as it would go. It was so hot and sultry, she wished Andrew had brought some of those air-conditioning units home with him.

It was too hot to sleep; Carly pushed aside first the coverlet and then the sheet, lying there in only her thin silk nightdress, but still uncomfortably hot. She thought of Kyle and wondered if he'd been hurt when he fell. She hoped that this time he would realise that it would be useless to contact her again and he would leave Grantston, because she didn't think she could stand to see him again. She heard Andrew go into his bedroom from the bathroom where he had been taking a long shower; to cool off from more than the heat, she supposed with unwanted cynicism. Now he would read for a while before turning off his light. She thought about him and what tomorrow would bring, but she didn't cry; she rather thought she was past crying. Turning over, she put her face into the pillow, trying to shut everything out of her mind and, although she didn't succeed, she at last drifted off to sleep.

She woke suddenly to full consciousness and was instantly aware that there was someone in the room. She lay still, thinking that it was Andrew, that he was unable to control himself and wait until tomorrow. Opening her eyes, she could see his outline over by the window. But it wasn't Andrew. The man who stood in the faint light of the waning moon loomed as tall as a giant. He was standing still, looking at her, but then Kyle moved silently towards the bed and stood by her. He didn't speak or attempt to touch her, but during those few moments Carly felt a surge of physical desire that was the deepest sexual experience she had ever known.

And Kyle must have felt it, too, because his voice was unsteady as he at last whispered her name. 'Carly?'

Slowly she sat up, unaware that her nightdress was clinging to her, outlining the curves of her slender body. 'Why have you come here?' She, too, kept her voice low.

'You know why; to find out why you've turned against me, why you sent me that letter.'

Dully, she said, 'It doesn't matter. It . . .'

'Of course it damn well matters,' Kyle replied, sounding all the more forceful because he had to keep his voice lowered. He sat down on the edge of the bed and reached out to take her hand, but Carly snatched it back.

'If you touch me I'll scream the place down,' she threatened.

His face tightened and he leaned back. 'All right, if that's the way you want it. Now tell me, everything.'

'Why tell you what you already know? I just feel sick at the way you used me. Pretending that you cared for

me when all the time you were trying to frighten
Andrew into buying you off. Is that how you manage to
live without working, Kyle? By extorting money from
people? By finding out where they're most vulnerable
and then hurting them?'

'So that's what Naughton told you? And you
believed him?'

'Why shouldn't I believe him? Andrew's never lied to
me.'

'Not until now. If what he told you was true, why did
he bother to make you write that letter to me? But your
own heart should have told you which of us to believe.
Doesn't it?' he added softly, reaching up a hand to
gently stroke her cheek.

But Carly immediately moved her head away before
he could touch her. 'I've already told you; it doesn't
matter. I'd decided never to see you again before
Andrew told me that he'd paid you to go away.'

Kyle slowly lowered his hand as he stared grimly at
her averted face. 'So you accepted the lies he told you
as an excuse to start hating me. To give yourself a
reason for denying that you love me.'

'I don't—love you.'

'Oh yes, you do. And you know it—or you would if
only you'd trust your own heart instead of being so
afraid.'

'Why shouldn't I be afraid of you?' she burst out, her
voice rising. 'You came along and messed up my whole
life. I could have lost everything.'

'But you have nothing here to lose,' Kyle said
harshly. 'Can't you see that? With me you have
everything to gain.'

For a long moment Carly gazed at his strong,
handsome face, shadowed in the soft light, then slowly
shook her head.

'It isn't too late,' he urged her. 'You could come with me now—or tomorrow. I'd come for you, you wouldn't have to be afraid.'

'No, I couldn't be that cruel to Andrew. You saw what a state he got into. He loves me. He couldn't live without me; he said so.'

'Of course he could,' Kyle interrupted impatiently. 'He's using moral blackmail again.'

Stubbornly Carly said, 'I don't care. It doesn't matter what you say; I'm—I'm going to marry him.'

'To sell yourself to him, you mean.'

'That isn't true!'

'Yes, it is. You're bartering your body in exchange for what you think is security and a family life, and you're doing it because Naughton says he loves you and you think you owe him.' He leaned forward urgently and this time she was unable to stop him taking hold of her wrists. 'But you don't owe him anything, Carly. He took you in because *he wanted to*, not because you asked him. The only person you owe anything to is yourself. To follow your heart and find happiness.'

'With you?' she exclaimed bitterly.

'Yes. Because I can give you that happiness. And because I love you.'

She stared at him, her eyes wide, then looked away. 'I can't. I have to marry Andrew.'

'Have to?' Kyle began scornfully, then suddenly his hands tightened on her wrists. 'Has he made you sleep with him as he threatened? Is that why?' he demanded harshly.

'That's none of your damn business!' Carly tried to pull her hands free, but he held on to them.

'Not my business, when a man forces himself on the girl I love?' Letting go her wrists, he took hold of her shoulders and pulled her towards him. 'Tell me the truth; have you slept with him?'

'No,' Carly admitted, her breath catching in her throat. 'Not yet.'

'But you're going to?'

'Oh, for heaven's sake, Kyle. I'm engaged to Andrew and I'm going to marry him in just a few weeks. I couldn't refuse him—even if I wanted to.'

'Do you want to?'

She stared at him, his face close to her own, then looked away.

'Do you?' he repeated urgently, his fingers pressing into her bare skin.

But she couldn't answer him. Shaking her head in despair, she begged, 'Oh, Kyle, please go away and leave me alone. Don't try to follow me or see me again. *Please!*'

Ignoring her plea, Kyle said, 'Why hasn't he made love to you already? What's he waiting for?'

Realising that he wouldn't leave it alone until he'd got an answer, Carly replied tonelessly, 'He won't here, not when his mother is in the house. He's going to take me back to my flat.'

'How romantic,' Kyle commented sardonically. 'When?'

She opened her mouth to answer, but heard a door open and footsteps in the corridor, then there was a sharp rap on her own door. 'Oh, my God!' She sat, frozen with horror, unable to think or move.

But Kyle reacted like lightning. 'Have you got a radio?' Dumbly she nodded and pointed, and he quickly turned the radio on and found a programme where two people were speaking, then he turned up the volume to just below normal conversation level. 'Tell him you couldn't sleep,' he instructed. Then he caught hold of her again. 'When?' he demanded urgently. 'When's he taking you to your flat?'

'What? Oh, tomorrow night.' Agitatedly Carly got out of bed as the knock came again and a voice said her name. 'Get out. Hurry!' she whispered frenziedly.

Kyle put a leg over the windowsill, grabbed the drainpipe and disappeared from view just as the door opened and Mrs Naughton came hesitantly into the room.

Looking round, she said, 'Is anything wrong? I thought I heard voices coming from this room.'

'Oh, I'm sorry,' Carly stammered, her heart thumping. 'It was so hot that I couldn't sleep and I turned on the radio. I'm sorry if it woke you.'

'You took a long time to open the door,' her hostess said suspiciously.

'I must have dozed off.' Going to the radio, Carly turned it off, hoping that by now Kyle had had time to get away. 'Even with all the windows open it's still hot, and so sultry.'

'Yes, I couldn't sleep either. I'm sorry I disturbed you, but I thought . . .' She broke off and shrugged. 'Well, goodnight.'

'Goodnight.'

Carly shut the door behind her and leant against it, thanking her stars for Kyle's quick thinking, although if Mrs Naughton had come straight into the room instead of knocking she would have been bound to see him. Carly wondered why she hadn't, then realised that the older woman had hesitated only because she thought that Andrew might have been with her. If she only knew!

Going to the window, Carly looked out into the garden, but there was no sign of Kyle, so she lay on her bed again, fully awake now, thinking about Kyle, and about the rash defiance he had shown by climbing into her room at night. If someone had seen him and called

the police—the thought made her go cold despite the
heat of the night. It had been a crazy thing to do.
Unless you were desperate, that was.

Nothing added up; not Kyle's behaviour nor
Andrew's. Surely Kyle wouldn't go this far to try and
get more money out of Andrew? Anyway, Andrew
wouldn't even know about it. And what Kyle had said
about the letter also made her start to think. If Kyle
really had taken money from Andrew to go away, there
would have been no point in wanting to tell him that
she didn't want to see him again. So there was the
possibility that Andrew, desperate at the thought of
losing her, had lied. But did it make any difference? It
still all boiled down to the question of what kind of
future she wanted. A lifetime of security and comfort
with Andrew, or an indefinite period of ecstasy on a
boat with Kyle. For even if she didn't know how long it
would last, Carly was quite certain that it would be
passionately ecstatic. But he had said that she was
afraid and it was true, she had to admit it. She didn't
know if she had the courage to entrust herself to Kyle,
to exchange security for uncertainty, to give up
everything she had for love.

From the moment she woke, late the next morning, it
was obvious that the weather was going to break. The
air was heavy, stifling, almost unbreathable. The sun
continued to beat down unmercifully, but there was an
ominousness in the sky that made everyone take in their
sun-loungers and put away their garden furniture and
parasols, their bright colours faded now by a month of
continuous sunshine. Carly woke feeling hot and sweaty
and stayed that way the whole day, even though she
wore only a pair of pants and a thin sundress. Even
when, at last, the sky darkened over completely and it
began to rain, it was still overbearingly hot.

Carly stood at her bedroom window and watched the
rain, reaching out an arm to let it fall on her and cool
her skin, but to her surprise the rain was warm. She
watched it for a long time, much as a person in a much
hotter climate would look bemused at the first rains
after years of drought, watching it hiss into steam on
the hot concrete, beat down the flowers and sink
gratefully into the cracks in the dried-up earth. A clock
chimed and, reluctantly, she began to change to go to
the flat with Andrew.

The windscreen wipers were on full speed and already
the gutters were starting to flood as they drove along,
the drains unable to cope with the onrush of water.
Most of the people they saw had umbrellas up, but the
rain was beating down so fiercely that they gave little
protection; and the rain was so warm that some people
had dispensed with them altogether, walking along
enjoying the rain with their light clothes clinging to
them, their hair plastered to their heads. Andrew held a
big golfing umbrella over them as they dashed from the
car to the flat, but even so the skirt of Carly's dress was
soaked by the time they got there.

They had already eaten at a restaurant, but Andrew
had brought a large bottle of champagne, whether to
make the occasion into some kind of ceremony or to
make her drunk, Carly didn't know or much care. She
was glad enough to have it and drank her first glass at a
gulp, more than willing to have her senses blunted. A
great clap of thunder reverberated through the room as
Andrew refilled her glass, drowning the toast he was
making. Lightning zigzagged across the sky, lighting the
room as bright as day. Carly turned with fascinated
eyes and would have gone to the window to watch, but
Andrew drew her back and began to kiss her. But he
had hardly touched her before the door-bell rang.

They looked at each other in surprise. 'Does anyone know you were coming here?' Andrew asked.

'No, of course not. Perhaps someone saw the light. Or it might be something to do with the storm. I'll go and see.'

'No, I'll go.'

Carly followed him to the door and watched as he went down the stairs, not really wondering about who was there, her thoughts all on what lay ahead. Andrew opened the front door and a woman immediately pushed past him, out of the rain. Others crowded in after her, and Carly's mouth opened in amazement as what seemed like a dozen people pushed into the tiny hallway, elbowing Andrew out of the way as they laughingly took off macs and closed umbrellas. Andrew was so squashed that he had to retreat up the stairs as people still came in the front door. The woman followed him, calling out a greeting to Carly as she came, and she saw with astonishment that it was Alison, the girl from the Crown and Anchor. In her hand, she carried a laden plastic bag of spicy-smelling food.

Andrew came angrily back into the sitting-room. 'What the hell are this lot doing here?'

Carly shook her head in bemusement. 'I've no idea.'

But then Alison and some of the others came into the room, faces she recognised from that night at the pub.

'Hi, Carly. We all went to the Green Dragon for a Chinese meal, but it was raining so hard that everyone else had the same idea and the place was full. So as you lived the nearest we decided to have a take-away and bring it here. Don't worry,' Alison laughed, 'we bought some for you. And there's enough for your—friend,' giving Andrew a sidelong glance full of curiosity. 'Plenty for everyone. And we've brought booze, too.

Although I see you've already got some. But ours isn't in the same class,' she remarked without envy, looking at the champagne bottle. 'Just cheap supermarket plonk. But it gets you just as drunk,' she added cheerfully.

She started to organise everyone, taking over the flat and sending people for plates and glasses as Carly and Andrew stood by, quite overpowered by the situation, and the rest of their uninvited guests crowded in. The last person to enter and shut the door firmly behind him was Kyle, his hair and shoulders wet from the rain. And then Carly saw it all. His blue eyes looked back at her mockingly as she gazed at him, his mouth twisted in a sardonic smile. And his unspoken message was clear.

CHAPTER EIGHT

CARLY stood quite still, looking at Kyle, but then Andrew saw him too and gave a snarl of anger and disbelief. 'Why, the damned, interfering . . .' He swung round on her. 'Did you know he was coming here?'

'No, of course not.' Carly turned away, feeling an insane desire to laugh, and went into the kitchen to help Alison find glasses and cutlery. When she came out Andrew and Kyle were still at opposite sides of the room, Andrew obviously furiously angry and Kyle, if Carly wasn't mistaken, enjoying the other man's anger.

Both men looked at her as she entered and Andrew made a curt gesture for her to join him, but Carly ignored it and went over to the table to talk to some of the others and help dish out the food.

'What will you and your friend have, Carly?' Alison asked her. 'Some spare ribs, or sweet and sour?'

'Thanks, but we ate earlier.'

'And hoped to have a quiet evening here together,' Andrew put in rudely. He came over to Carly and caught her arm. 'Can't you get rid of them?' he demanded, hardly bothering to lower his voice. But no one took any notice. There wasn't enough room at the table, so people were sitting on the settee and on the floor, their plates perched on their knees, talking as they ate, so there was enough noise to cover his rudeness.

'Of course not,' Carly replied in a sharp undertone. 'If you don't like it, you'd better go home.'

'Good idea. We'll leave them to it.'

'I said *you* go, Andrew. I'm staying.'

His jaw tightened. 'Do you think I'd leave you here alone with that—that scoundrel?'

'I'm hardly alone!' Her sweeping gesture embraced all the other people in the room.

'You know damn well what I mean. I'm not leaving while he's here.'

Carly shrugged. 'Suit yourself. Though what you expect him to try with all these people here, I can't imagine. Can you?'

'It's probably just another ruse to try and get more money out of me.'

Carly raised her head to look him straight in the eye. 'So you say,' she commented coldly.

Immediately he looked away and began to attack her. 'You oughtn't to have let them in. If they think they can come here they might try pushing their way into The Elms.'

'Are you saying they wouldn't be welcome there?'

'What, this rabble?' Andrew gave a sardonic, disbelieving laugh.

Her face hardening, Carly said sharply, 'These are extremely clever and artistic people who are working by using their own talents, not living like a leech on the backs of others! And they happen to be my friends.'

Andrew stared at her for a moment as if he couldn't believe his ears, then he turned abruptly away and strode over to an unoccupied corner where he leant against the wall, his arms folded, face grim. Carly looked after him and knew that she ought to feel remorseful, but found instead that she didn't much care.

No one seemed in any hurry to leave. The rain still drummed violently against the windowpanes and the claps of thunder were right overhead for a long time, shaking the old building to its foundations. Carly sat around, talking to several people, but she made no attempt to go near Kyle, who was squatting on the floor over by the door and seemed content to stay there. Andrew, however, grew more impatient by the minute. Eventually the storm seemed to ease a little and one or two people made a move to go which turned into a mass exodus, Kyle leaving with them.

Carly ignored Andrew's frown and went down to the front door to say goodnight to them all, but couldn't stop her eyes frequently straying to Kyle as he came down the stairs behind the others, waiting as they put on macs and scarves and sorted out which umbrella was whose. At last he reached her and took her hand, drawing her to one side.

'Are you angry with me?'

She shook her head. 'No.'

'Good. That's something at least.' Then, suddenly impatient, 'Why are you letting him use you like this?'

Carly took her hand away. 'He wasn't taking anything from me that I wasn't willing to give.'

'You might be *willing* to give yourself to him out of mistaken feelings of gratitude and loyalty, but you're a hell of a long way from being eager. For God's sake, Carly, come to your senses before it's too late!'

'I wasn't aware that I was out of my senses,' she observed coldly.

'How can you be so damned dispassionate!' Kyle exclaimed exasperatedly, then his jaw tightened. 'Or is it that I've been wrong about you all along? Is it really his money that you're marrying him for, after all? Is that it?'

Her face paled. 'Get out of here, Kyle!'

'And leave the two of you alone to complete your coldblooded mating? For you sure as hell couldn't call

it making love—you selling and him buying,' he
sneered.

Anger flooded her cheeks and she lifted a hand to hit
him across the face, but he anticipated her and caught
her wrist. 'You swine! How dare you speak to me like
that!'

'That's better. At least you're giving way to your
feelings—even if they are only anger.' But then his voice
grew urgent. 'Leave him, Carly. Come with me. I can
give you love that you never even dreamed of.'

Carly glared at him, her chest heaving, and said on a
sob of fury, 'I've had just about as much as I can take! I
wouldn't go with you if you were the last man on earth.
Now get out of here! Go on, get out!' She snatched her
wrist from his suddenly slack fingers, and pushed his
huge bulk towards the open door, taking him by
surprise so that he obeyed her.

But once outside he put his hands on the door frame
so that she couldn't shut it. 'Carly . . .'

'Get out of here. Get out of my life!' she yelled at
him, and slammed the door to so that he had to leap
backwards to avoid getting his fingers crushed.

'Well done!' Andrew exclaimed from the top of the
stairs where he'd been listening to the end of their
argument. 'I'm glad you've given that rogue his come-
uppance at last. We shouldn't see any more of him,' he
added with satisfaction.

He went to take her in his arms as Carly came back
upstairs, but she pushed past him and went into the
bedroom. He followed her, a pleased smile on his face.
'Darling, I'm so pleased you've seen him for what he is.
We might as well stay here the whole night now. We
can make love till morning,' he said thickly, coming up
behind her and putting his hands under her arms to try
to caress her breasts as she opened the wardrobe.

'Oh no, we can't. We're leaving,' she answered shortly, pushing his hands away and taking a suitcase from the wardrobe and beginning to fill it with the rest of her clothes.

'Leaving? But why? Now that we've got rid of that crowd of layabouts we can go to bed together.' But she didn't answer him and went on putting clothes into her case. 'Carly,' he demanded peremptorily.

'Don't yell at me as if I were a dog, Andrew. I said we're leaving and I meant it.' Closing the case, she carried it into the sitting-room and hesitated, looking round at all the dirty china and glasses, then shrugged, 'Oh, to hell with it.'

The rain had eased a little as they came outside, but it was still hot and sultry. There was the distant rumble of thunder as if the storm they had just had was only a prelude and the heavens were gathering their strength for another onslaught on their enemy the earth. Rainwater ran down the middle of the mews like a mountain stream, forming pools wherever there was a drain, and both of them had wet feet by the time they reached the car.

'If we'd stayed at the flat we'd have avoided all this,' grumbled Andrew, surveying his soaking handmade leather shoes.

'Why don't you stop moaning, Andrew, and drive?'

His mouth drawing into a thin line, Andrew started the car and drove in a resentful silence, although the roads were already half-flooded in places and he had to go very slowly. They reached The Elms just as the phone was ringing and he hurried inside to answer it, while Carly went up to her room.

He rejoined her a few minutes later and there was a pleased note in his voice as he said, 'That was Mother. She's over at the Martin sisters' place and doesn't want to risk driving home in the storm, so she's going to spend the night there.'

'Didn't she want you to go and pick her up?' asked Carly, collecting up all her dress designs and placing the drawings carefully in a portfolio.

'No, she said she didn't want me to risk going out on a night like this. So we have the house to ourselves, with no danger of those damned hippies coming round. What are you doing?' he asked, noticing for the first time.

'I'm packing up my things.'

'Why? You don't expect me to let you go back to the flat after tonight, do you?'

'Whether you *let* me or not doesn't come into it,' she answered tartly. 'But as it happens I'm not going back to the flat. I'm leaving.'

'Leaving? But where ... My God, you're going to go to Anderson after all! What the hell are you playing at? Less than an hour ago you threw him out of the door.' His voice rose in anger. 'How can you possibly throw yourself away on a good-for-nothing like that when I have so much to offer you? And I've made you what you are, don't forget that. If it wasn't for Mother and me you'd be just a common little chit out of an orphanage. You owe everything to us!'

Carly stared at him for a moment, then deliberately took her suitcase down from the top of the wardrobe and began to throw the few things she had brought with her to The Elms into it.

'Are you listening to me?' Andrew shouted at her. 'You needn't think you can come crawling back here when he throws you out. I'm not going to take his leavings!'

Slamming her case shut, Carly rounded on him. 'That's all you care about, isn't it—who has me first? I thought you loved me, Andrew, but since Kyle came along I've found out that all you really want me for is sex—that and to have a wife half your age to flaunt in front of all your so-called friends. Somebody you've moulded into the kind of person to fit in with your lifestyle—your status.' Picking up the case and her portfolio, she went on, 'Well, as it happens you're wrong; I'm not going to Kyle. And I'm not going to marry you either. I'm sick and tired of having people tell me how I should lead my life, what I should or shouldn't do. From now on I'm going to make my own choices, my own decisions. And I'm going to start by leaving here and going somewhere where I can be myself!' And she marched out of the room and down the stairs.

Andrew ran after her. 'You can't be serious! You'll never manage on your own. How will you live? You don't have any money left!'

'I'll manage.' Carly reached the front door and pulled it open.

'You won't be able to set up in business again without me to help you and back you.'

'Then I'll do something else. Anything.'

'And where do you think you're going to live?' he shouted. 'You won't be able to get a flat like the one you've got now, you know. I had to pull a few strings before you got that. *And* I've been subsidising the rent.'

Reaching her Mini, Carly turned to look at him. It was still raining heavily and they were both wet. 'Thanks,' she said bitterly. 'You just proved to me how right I am to go.' She threw her things into the back, then went over to Andrew's car to get her other suitcase.

'I'm not going to let you go,' he yelled at her above the noise of the rain. 'You're mad! You'll regret this by tomorrow!'

'Maybe I will. But at least I'll be free. Free to give myself to whoever I want, not in payment for something I never asked for.'

Andrew glared at her furiously, the rain running down his face into his collar. 'All right then, go. Go to hell for all I care! Become the common little slut you were meant to be if I hadn't taken you out of the gutter. But don't think you can ever come back to Grantston. If you do I'll ruin you—I swear it!'

Carly gave him one long look of open contempt. 'You're a lousy loser, Andrew.' Then she took her case over to the Mini, got in and drove away without a backward glance.

She took the road to the east, not much caring where she was going but automatically following the main road towards London. Feeling too angry and bitter to be sad, she drove with a set face as she concentrated on negotiating the wet roads, not hurrying because of the bad weather. She felt used and dirty, like a bone that two dogs had fought over, each obsessed with their own greed. Well, now she was free of both of them: of the man who wanted to exploit her and the man who offered her only an aimless existence.

At first she felt bitterly resentful towards Kyle; as she'd been afraid ever since he'd come on the scene, she had lost everything she possessed: her home, her business, her future. But as the distance between herself and Grantston increased some of the bitterness faded and she began to see that he had done her a favour. Some time in the future she would have seen through Andrew, but by then it would have been too late, she would have become part of his life, one of his possessions, and he would never have let her go. Carly could almost imagine what would have happened to her: the gradual disillusionment turning to hatred, the search for solace and love in other men, or drink—even drugs. She had read of and even, in one or two cases, met such women and in her youth and ignorance had despised them, but now she saw just how easily you could make the first mistake that would lead to becoming one of those unhappy people. But at least Kyle had saved her from that, even if he had no alternative to offer—except love.

She drove on through the dark night. It was still raining, but she had outdistanced the worst of the storms and it was simply rain, not the pent-up downpour of a month of drought. And there was no moon now; the midsummer moon had been drowned out of existence. After a couple of hours she noticed that the fuel was getting low and pulled into the next garage. She paid by credit card and went inside the attendant's booth to wait while he filled in the form. He had the radio switched on to the local late night music programme, but it was interrupted by a news flash. 'We interrupt this programme to warn all motorists travelling towards the Grantston and Appleby area of serious flooding. The River Rib has burst its banks and part of the town and most of the approach roads are flooded. The storm has caused widespread havoc, bringing down trees and tearing a great many boats from their moorings. Several boats have been carried down river and wrecked on the Grantston Weir. It is feared that lives may have been lost as there were several holiday craft among them.'

''Ere, miss. It's ready for you to sign.' The attendant pushed the credit card slip under Carly's nose.

'Did—did you hear that?' She stared at him wide-eyed, unable to take it in.

'Hear what?'

'That news bulletin. It said Grantston, didn't it? That boats had been wrecked there?'

'Dunno. I wasn't really listening.'

'Have you got a phone here?'

'Yes, it's over there.' He gestured towards a booth on the other side of the forecourt. 'Sign this first, though.'

Hurriedly Carly scribbled her name, then ran over to the booth, dialling Directory Enquiries to get the number of the radio station, then asking to speak to someone about their news bulletin. Two minutes later her worst fears were confirmed. Dropping the receiver, she ran out to the Mini, started it and turned in the direction she had come, back to Grantston.

She drove fast now, pushing the little car to its limit, trying to concentrate her mind entirely on getting back as quickly as possible, but always at the back of her mind was the chill dread of what she might find when she got there. Luckily the rain had kept most of the traffic off the roads and she got to within a few miles of Grantston in record time, but then a lot of lights appeared on the road ahead and a policeman holding a storm lantern waved her to a standstill.

'Sorry, miss, you won't be able to go any further along this road tonight.'

'But I've got to. I've got to get to Grantston.'

He shook his head and raindrops flew from his cap on to the waterproof cape covering his uniform. 'Not on this road you won't. There's a tree down and half a mile past that the road's completely flooded.'

'What roads are open, then?' she demanded, her voice sharp with worry.

'You could try going back to the crossroads and then cutting across country to the Bath road; that might still be usable.'

'Thanks.' Carly immediately turned the car and

headed that way, but the connecting road was much smaller and more winding, hardly more than a country lane, so she had to go much slower, cursing at the waste of time. But even though she went as fast as she could, she was still too late; that road, too, was impassable. Swearing under her breath, her heart torn by anxiety, Carly turned the car, the water half-way up the wheels, and headed for another road she knew of. This one, when she reached it twenty minutes later, luckily seemed clear. Putting her foot down, Carly drove as fast as she dared in the rain and darkness. Her headlights cut swathes of light, but then another electric storm burst overhead and she had jagged, awesome flashes of lightning that tore the sky apart to help light her way, followed by blinding darkness as the earth waited in trepidation for the thunder to burst and torrential rain to fall.

But even so, she made good speed and could see the lights of the town below as she breasted the top of a small hill. Every light in the place seemed to be on; no one would be sleeping tonight. With a sigh of thankfulness, Carly put her foot on the accelerator and drove down the hill into the valley. The road stretched ahead of her, long and straight and empty. Then a great roaring noise filled her ears, coming from the right. It sounded like a train or an aeroplane, but couldn't possibly be. She tried to look out of the side window, but it was impossible to see anything through the rain. The great roar of sound became louder and she gave a sob of fright, putting her foot down hard on the accelerator in fear, her hands gripping the steering-wheel.

The wall of water that flooded across the valley as the river burst its banks at the upper reach picked up the Mini as if it was an unwanted toy and threw it aside, leaving it behind as the muddy waters rushed across the fields, uprooting any bushes and small trees in their path.

Carly screamed, hanging on to the steering-wheel as the car was tossed from side to side, but fortunately it stayed upright and her safety-belt saved her from anything more than being badly bruised. When it came to a standstill she wanted to go on screaming, sure that something worse was going to happen, but the gradual diminishing of the roar of water slowly reassured her that she was safe. Or comparatively safe. As she sat there water began to fill the car and was soon above her knees. Hastily she undid her strap, realising that she would have to get out, that the level of flood water was rising as more came from up river. When she couldn't open the door against the pressure of water, she almost panicked, but then common sense came to her aid and she wound down the window, more water immediately surging in. Grabbing up her handbag, she scrambled out of the window and up on to the roof.

There was no question of being able to walk or swim back to higher ground; the water swirled too dangerously and was full of mud and uprooted trees. She would just have to sit tight and hope that it wouldn't get any higher, but it was quite some time before she was satisfied that it had reached its peak, just a couple of inches below the roof of the Mini, and that she was safe for the time being. So then all she had to do was sit and wait for someone to come and rescue her. And wonder frenziedly whether Kyle was alive or dead.

It was almost eight o'clock the next morning before Carly was rescued. The parts of her that hadn't been wet from the flood waters had soon been soaked by the rain, but at least it was summer and although wet, she

hadn't been too cold. It had been about five before the
rain had stopped and she'd been left in the darkness to
listen to the waters gurgling around the car, which
sometimes rocked frighteningly when a big tree root or
branch bumped into it. She sat there for what seemed
like interminable days, her anxious imagination picturing all sorts of terrible things; but the human brain can
only take so much and in the end she sat in numb
impatience, the pictures of Kyle being drowned in the
weir or swallowed up in a sea of mud pushed to the
back of her mind.

When it grew light enough for her to look around
her, Carly saw that the Mini had been swept off the
road on to the verge and was perched rather
precariously on a low bank, which had probably saved
it from being covered completely. Gingerly she stood up
to get a better view, and was appalled at what she saw:
it was impossible now to make out the original course
of the river, it had spread right across the fields beside it
on either side and there were only the tops of bushes
poking out of the water to tell where the hedges were.
The road she had been travelling on was completely
under water, filled now by a traffic of broken trees and
debris that floated slowly by in water that was more like
soft, oozing mud and smelt rank and fetid. Once the
carcass of a poor dead cow went by some distance
away, and Carly turned away in horror, those pictures
instantly coming back into her mind.

The only sign of habitation was a largish house about
a hundred yards or so away. It seemed deserted and she
thought that the owners had probably abandoned it
and gone to safety, but a couple of hours later she
spotted a movement at one of the windows and stood
up again to shout and wave. She wasn't sure whether
anyone had seen her until an hour or so later when a

police Range Rover came into sight, travelling very slowly down what had once been the road. By then the water had subsided a great deal and was mostly foul-smelling mud that came up over the floor of the car. When they got near enough the Range Rover stopped and a burly policeman wearing waterproof waders up to his waist, got out and plodded over to her, his feet making loud sucking noises in the mud every time he took a step. His face broke into a pleased grin when he saw that he had an attractive young girl to rescue.

'The people in that house over there phoned us about you. How long have you been here?' he asked her.

'All night. I was trying to get back to Grantston.' She gazed at him with large, anxious eyes, her body trembling. 'The boats that went over the weir; was—was anyone drowned?'

Seeing her worry, he answered, 'Somebody you care about on a boat was there?'

'Yes. The boat's called the *Lydia*. It's a narrow boat, a barge. Painted red and black. There's—there's a man on it.'

'Well, that figures. But I couldn't tell you, love. You'd better let me take you over to the car and then we'll radio headquarters for you to find out.' Reaching up, he picked her up and carried her over to the Range Rover, depositing her neatly in the front seat beside his grinning colleague, then he turned to go back, but Carly stopped him. 'What about your suitcases?'

'Oh, leave them,' she said impatiently. 'Everything in them must all be ruined anyway.'

'All right.' He got in beside her so that she was squashed between the two men, which they didn't seem to mind at all. 'Is it your car?' the policeman asked her, looking across at the Mini. 'It's going to be a hell of a job to get that fit to go back on the road. But you'll have to arrange for a garage to come and shift it as soon as possible.'

Carly had a flash of inspiration. 'No, it isn't my car. It belongs to Mr Andrew Naughton of The Elms in Highwood Road. If you'll contact him, he'll take care of everything.'

He gave her a curious look. 'Lent it to you, did he?'

'Something like that. Could we radio your station now, please?' she asked, unable to control her anxiety any longer.

They did as she asked, in the meantime driving slowly towards Grantston, the high vehicle able to clear the mud, although now and again they had to stop while the man with waders got out and cleared tree branches and other debris from their path. It was some time before they got an answer to her query, and even then it only served to increase her anxiety. Four bodies had been recovered from the weir so far, three of them men. At least six boats had gone over, but the water there was still so fierce that it had been impossible for divers to go down and identify and search them, but it was known that one was a narrow boat because someone had seen it go, but they couldn't remember the name. The only crumb of comfort was that several of the boats were thought to have been empty.

It took nearly two nail-biting hours to cover the two miles into Grantston. During that time the sun came out and shone as brightly as it had before the thunderstorm, giving the landscape an unreal, hellish aspect, as if the earth had been blasted open in a battle. And when they reached the town, that, too, looked as if everyone was clearing up after a war. Every window and door was open as people cleaned their houses of the terrible mud. The streets were full of council workers and helpers, shifting debris, trying to unblock drains, turning on emergency water supplies. Parts of the town, of course, had escaped completely, those on the higher ground like the big houses in the area around The Elms and the new estate of houses on the Bristol Road. The old Market Hall, too, had escaped, for the simple reason that some inspired townsmen in the sixteenth century had decided to build it on high pillars so that the market stalls could trade beneath its shelter.

The policemen dropped her off as near to the weir as they could and she ran through the streets, the mud splashing unheeded up her legs. There was a crowd of people round the weir, reporters, TV cameramen and lots of police and officials as well as the usual inevitable crowd of avid sensation-seekers. Carly pushed her way through them and stopped, aghast at what she saw. Boats were smashed down on top of one another as if deliberately thrown there by some giant hand. Some weren't even under water now but were upside down on the smashed hulls and superstructures of other boats. Over them all poured the muddied waters of the weir that thundered down its steep bank in unstoppable ferocity, making it impossible for the frogmen who stood by helplessly to go down and search the wrecks of what had once been beautiful, cared-for craft. But Carly's eyes were riveted to a black hull that protruded, upside down, a little way out of the water, its narrowness making it unmistakably a barge. There was a gaping hole in it and it was mostly submerged, held down by the weight of a big cabin cruiser that had come over the weir on top of it. It was impossible to see what colour it was painted under the muddy water.

Somebody spoke to her, but she didn't take it in, then someone took hold of her arm. 'Are you all right, miss? You oughtn't to be here. This isn't the place for rubberneckers,' the man added scathingly.

Numbly she turned and saw a man in some sort of uniform. 'That boat—the—the narrow boat,' she stammered. 'Do you—oh, *please*, do you know the name of it?'

Seeing her distress, he was immediately concerned, his voice sympathetic as he shook his head. 'Sorry, no. And we won't be able to find out until we manage to put a temporary dam across the weir. They're bringing that by road from Bristol now, but it will be hours before it gets here and we get it erected. We might not even be able to get down there until tomorrow.' He patted her arm. 'Why don't you go home and phone up the police station? If you give them your number they'll get in touch with you as soon as they know anything. Somebody close to you on the boat, is there?' he asked sympathetically.

Carly looked back at the broken hull. 'Somebody who could have been very close,' she answered on a murmur of despair. 'If only I'd let him.'

She turned away, walking dazedly through the streets, knowing in her heart that there would be no hope for anyone trapped in the broken boats, they would have been drowned hours ago by the river—or the mud. They had already found the bodies of three men, which would, she supposed, have been taken to the local hospital. But her heart shrank from going there to enquire—to see. Her only hope now was that it hadn't been the *Lydia* or that Kyle hadn't been on board, but she couldn't imagine him leaving the boat to its fate, he would stay on to the bitter end, desperately trying to save it. Turning her footsteps towards the other end of town where the warehouses were situated, Carly began to hurry, then to run again.

The sun was shining full on to the Crown and Anchor. The doors were open and the forecourt in front of it full of tables, chairs and carpets that had been brought out to dry. A man was sweeping mud out of the saloon bar, but it wasn't Kyle. Carly recognised the landlady hanging curtains on a makeshift line, but didn't stop to question her, instead running through the mud pool that had once been the garden round to the back of the pub.

There was a boat tied up there. It was painted red and black with the gay castles and garlands of flowers traditional on narrow boats. A man was working on it, cleaning down the mud-splattered deck with a mop. He was dressed in ragged denim shorts and a tee-shirt, very tall and strong, his fair hair like gold under the sun.

Carly leant against the wall of the pub, her body suddenly too weak to move, her mind and heart one long hosanna of relief and thankfulness. She gazed at Kyle, almost unable to believe that he was safe, that the long night of fear had been groundless.

As if feeling her eyes on him, he glanced up and saw her. An incredulous look came into his eyes, but then he gave a huge leap on to the bank and ran over to her. He stopped a yard away as they stared at each other, but then Carly gave a small sob and ran into his arms.

They both spoke at once.

'Oh God, I thought you were dead! I thought you'd gone over the weir.'

'Where have you been? What happened to you? They told me you'd gone away.'

'Oh, Kyle!' Carly put her hands up to his face, assuring herself that he was real, tears rolling down her cheeks. 'I've been such a fool. Why didn't you make me listen to you? I love you so much. I couldn't bear it if anything happened to you.'

He stared at her, unable to believe his ears, then he gave a great shout of happiness, lifting her up high in

the air. 'At last! I've been waiting and longing to hear
you say that from the moment I met you.' Then he
lowered her until her head was level with his and kissed
her, his arms hugging her close to him, moulding her
body against his own.

When at last he released her mouth Carly stared at
him dazedly. 'You mean you loved me, right from the
first?'

'Of course I did. From the moment you fell in the
river and I hauled you out looking like a drowned rat.'
Setting her on her feet, he looked at her critically. 'You
don't look much unlike one now. What happened to
you? When I tried to phone you this morning,
Naughton said you'd gone away. I didn't believe him
and went up there to find you, but his mother showed
me your empty room and that the Mini was gone. I
didn't believe Naughton, but I believed his mother,' he
added on a note of compelled respect. 'Where did you
go? I didn't know where to start searching for you.'

'I was heading for London,' Carly admitted. 'I just
wanted to get away, to give myself a chance to think.
But then I heard on the radio about the boats going
over the weir. And—and all my thinking was
crystallised into one second. Oh, Kyle, I was so afraid
for you!' Putting her arms as far round him as they
would go, she hugged him tightly, her face pressed into
his chest.

He held her close, letting her feel the comfort of his
strength and nearness, his hand stroking her hair. 'No,
the *Lydia* was quite safe. I know how to tie a boat to
weather a storm, even one as bad as last night's. I take
it you turned round and came back again?'

She nodded, 'Yes. But the river broke its banks and I
got stranded. I wasn't rescued until this morning.'
Freeing herself, she took a step backwards and looked

up at him uncertainly. 'Kyle, I lost everything. All my
clothes, my portfolio. All I have is the furniture and a
few things back at my flat.'

He smiled and her heart jumped about three
somersaults. 'Good,' he said softly, 'I wouldn't want
you any other way.' His eyes held hers, so blue, so
loving, Carly's insides started to melt and she didn't
know how she'd ever resisted him. 'Right now,' he told
her, looking at the mud on her legs, 'you need a
shower.'

'I suppose I do,' she agreed reluctantly. 'I'll go back
to the flat and . . .'

Kyle took hold of her hand. 'There's a perfectly good
shower on the boat.'

Her breath caught in her throat as she looked into his
eyes and read their message. 'Why—why yes, so there
is.' And she let him lead her down into the cabin.

He undressed her slowly, his eyes openly admiring
her slim figure, and he washed her even more slowly,
his hands gently cleaning away the mud and dirt of her
long night of fear. Then he dried her very tenderly, his
eyes darkening with need as he touched her.

Carly's body trembled a little, but with desire and
eager anticipation, not from fear. She would never be
afraid, not of this big giant of a man who had finally
won her. And she would never again be afraid of facing
life, of giving and accepting love. Picking her up in his
arms, Kyle carried her into his cabin and laid her down
on his bunk in the sunlight streaming through the
window, stood looking down at her waiting for him for
a long moment before lying down beside her.

'I love you,' he told her. 'I'll never stop loving you
until the day I die.' His mouth took hers, gently at first
but with rapidly growing passion that overwhelmed her.
And Carly surrendered to it, just as she surrendered her

body in ecstatic love and glorious happiness to her Viking invader.

They lay together, some hours later, their damp bodies entwined, for the moment physically satiated. Carly ran her fingers along Kyle's chest, feeling the soft dew of perspiration. 'I'd never have believed it could be like this,' she said softly. 'Not after the way Andrew . . .'

Kyle put a finger over her lips. 'Forget about him; he's the past, we're the future.'

She kissed his finger, then bit the tip gently. 'But we must leave here. I couldn't stay here now.'

'Of course. Just as soon as we settle all your affairs.'

'If you mean the flat, forget it. I don't care about it any more.'

'You should; it was the only thing that was really yours.'

Carly shook her head. 'No, Andrew told me, just before I left, that he'd arranged for me to get it and that he'd even been subsidising the rent,' she said bitterly.

Understanding how she felt, Kyle lifted a hand to gently push away a strand of hair from her damp forehead. 'Look, Alison and her boy-friend are looking for a flat, why don't you let them have it and do a deal over the furniture? They'd love a place like that.'

'Could they afford it?'

'I think so, they're both working.'

'Okay, we'll find them and ask them.'

'Mm,' Kyle agreed, his mouth coming down to kiss her breast. 'But later.'

Carly gasped. 'Wh-when are you going to shave off that beard?'

'Don't you like it?' His voice was muffled.

'It tickles.' His mouth moved over her. 'But—but perhaps I do quite like it.'

He laughed, lifting his head to look at her. 'Maybe I'll shave it off—after we're married.'

Carly's eyes widened and her mouth dropped open. 'We—we're going to get married?'

'Well, of course we are.' He looked indignant. 'You don't think I'm going to let you lead me into a life of sin, do you? I've heard about girls like you. Leading us poor men astray and then refusing to marry them, throwing Women's Lib in their faces. It's marriage or nothing.' He raised a quizzical, mocking eyebrow. 'Okay?'

Her eyes misty, Carly gazed up at him happily. 'Why—why yes, that's fine.'

'Good. Then we'll do it just as soon as it can be arranged.'

He bent to kiss her again, but Carly said, 'Kyle, did you make any promises to Andrew? After that night you walked away from my flat together, he said that you'd promised him that you'd go away.'

'Was that when I was supposed to have demanded money from him?' She nodded and he went on, 'It was completely the other way round. He offered me money to leave, to stay away from you. When I refused he began to beg and plead, saying how much he needed you, how much you meant to him. Always his own feelings and needs, never yours. He even cried,' he added in angry disgust. 'In the end I promised to give him the next day to sort things out with you. He was so pathetic.' His mouth twisted.

'But you didn't give him a whole day. That night you rang and came round, until Andrew sent for the police.'

He gave her a wicked grin. 'The daytime was one thing, the night was another.' His face changed, becoming grim. 'I couldn't bear to think of you with him. Of him touching you. Taking your youth, your loveliness.'

Quickly she reached to take his hand. 'It doesn't matter. Only now matters. My body was never alive until now. Until you.'

'Sweetheart!' He kissed her again and soon they were lost to everything but love, until an hour or so later when Carly said languidly, 'Kyle, just how much *did* Andrew offer you to stay away from me?' And she fell asleep with Kyle's laughter in her ears.

There was a coolness in the air. Carly could feel it as she carried her basket of milk and eggs across the field. It was quite early one morning in mid-September and she had walked up from where the boat was moored to the farm they could see in the distance to buy them. She paused, knee-high in a meadow of tall grass and bright red poppies and looked down to where the *Lydia* was tied to the river bank. The sun still shone, but it had lost its summer heat.

They had been married for over a month. A simple ceremony in a registrar's office in Bristol which was a far cry from the huge wedding that Andrew had planned, but which had meant so much, so very much more. Carly hadn't seen Andrew again or been in touch with him, and if she thought of him it was only with pity; she had no regrets. She had pushed the future out of her mind and was supremely happy. The past was almost forgotten; she felt as if she hadn't begun to live until she met Kyle. And she had found that he was indeed a giant of a man, in every way. Her body felt empty without him.

Carly chuckled at herself, at how she had changed. Now she did her own hair instead of going to the hairdressers every week and it looked just as good.

Her skin was tanned a deep brown from being always
in the open, and she wore a simple shirt and shorts,
her feet bare in the soft grass. She couldn't, for the
moment, remember the last time she'd worn a pair of
shoes. Kyle had said when he first met her that she
was the country girl type, and he had been proved
right; she had happily shed her sophisticated image.
She saw Kyle come on to the deck and wave to her,
then start walking towards her. Carly ran down the
field to meet him, the breeze in her hair.

But as she reached him she stopped short in
astonishment. 'You've shaved off your beard!' She
looked at him, head on one side, seeing his strong
determined jawline for the first time. 'Not bad,' she said
critically. 'At least it wasn't hiding a double chin.'

He grinned at her and put up a hand to stroke his
smooth skin. 'It always feels peculiar for the first couple
of days.'

'Why have you shaved it off? I mean, why now?'

Kyle gave her a rather odd look. 'Because it's time to
go home. The summer's over.'

'Home? I don't understand. The *Lydia* is our home.'

'For the summer, yes. But the rest of the year my
home is in Oxford. I have a house there. And I work
there.' He waited for her to say something, but Carly
could only stare at him speechlessly. So he went on, 'At
the university. As an assistant professor of mathematics.
You see, I'm an—er—physicist.' He broke off, looking
at her half warily, half in concern as she continued to
just stand and gaze at him speechlessly. 'Carly?'

She came slowly to life. 'Why didn't you tell me?'

'Because you were so hooked on security that I
wanted you to be sure just what your feelings were
about me. I didn't want you to . . .'

'You louse!' Galvanised into sudden action, Carly

took an egg from her basket and threw it at him. 'You rotten, deceiving pig!'

The rest of the eggs followed in quick succession as Kyle put up his hands to try and defend himself. When she ran out of ammunition he ran and caught her, falling to the ground as she struggled with him. 'You wildcat!' Catching her arms, he held them on either side of her head as he half lay on top of her. 'Forgive me?'

'No, I don't,' Carly returned furiously. 'I suppose you're stinking rich. You swine!'

He gave a shout of laughter. 'No, but I've enough to take us to find the Golden Road to Samarkand. Or down a different river next summer. Whatever you want.' He bent to kiss her and it felt strange without his beard. 'Did you really believe that I'd marry you without being able to provide for you, for our children?'

'I didn't care. I just wanted to be with you.' She put her arms around his neck. 'I'll miss you while you're working.'

'But we'll be together most of the time. And you'll be able to start your business up again. There are lots of shops in Oxford that would take your clothes.'

Carly smiled up at him rather tremulously, then sighed, 'Do we really have to go there now?'

''Fraid so. There's a marina a few miles down the river where we'll leave the *Lydia*. Then we'll take my car and drive back to Oxford.'

Turning her head, Carly looked at the boat. 'I shall miss it. I've been so happy on board her—with you.'

Kyle smiled and began to undo the buttons of her shirt. 'We still have a few hours,' he observed, a wickedly suggestive glint in his blue eyes.

'Oughtn't we to go on the boat?' Carly asked with a little gasp as he began to fondle her.

'This grass is very long,' he pointed out, his voice husky.

Her astonished look changed to a smile as she drew him down to her. After all, what else would you expect of a Viking?